# ✦ AUTOGRAPH PAGE ✦

Mike McPhail

Danielle Ackley-McPhail

Greg Schauer

FT'ARC

THE DIE IS CAST

EDITED BY
GREG SCHAUER

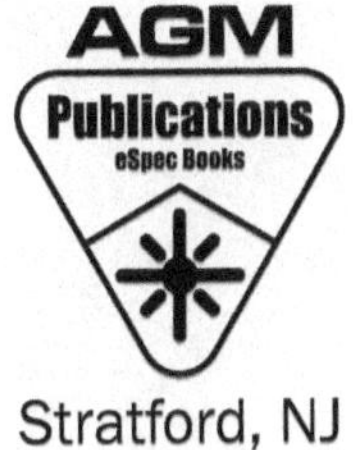

Stratford, NJ

PUBLISHED BY
AGM Publications,
an imprint of eSpec Books LLC
Danielle McPhail, Publisher
PO Box 493,
Stratford, New Jersey 08084
www.especbooks.com

ISBN: 978-1-942990-24-6
ISBN (ebook): 978-1-942990-25-3

Design: Mike and Danielle McPhail
Cover Art Background:
Sci fi futuristic user interface © mikser45, www.shutterstock.com©
Cover Art Design and Icon: © Mike McPhail
www.mikemcphail.com
www.milscifi.com

This book is dedicated to
the first Parr Scout

Bandit McPhail
"Colonel Mau"

1974 to 1992

If you would know a man,
observe how he treats a cat.
Robert A. Heinlein

Special thanks to these early play testers and dear friends, we miss you all.

Kenneth Brandt
Lennart Olsson
Edwin Pineiro
Gustov Ahumada
Jeffrey Ponce
Victor Ponce
Toni Severon
Lourdes Severon
Larry Francis
Ivan Borges
Esteban Nunez
Kerstin Olsson
Dewey Samanc
Luis Valazquez II
Danielle Ackley

ACKNOWLEDGEMENTS

Earlier versions of the following stories were originally published as indicated:

"Wayward Child"by Mike McPhail, *Breach the Hull*, edited by Mike McPhail, Marietta Publishing, 2006; Dark Quest Books, 2009.

"Chimera" by Mike McPhail, *No Longer Dreams*, edited by Danielle Ackley-McPhail, L. Jagi Lamplighter, Lee C. Hillman, and Jeffrey Lyman, Light Circle Books, 2005.

"Fun and Games" by Danielle Ackley-McPhail, *Best Laid Plans* (DTF5) edited by Mike McPhail, Dark Quest Books, 2013.

'Cling Peaches"by Mike McPhail, *So it Begins*, edited by Mike McPhail, Dark Quest Books, 2009.

"In the Dying Light" by Danielle Ackley-McPhail, *Breach the Hull* (DTF1) edited by Mike McPhail, Marietta Publishing, 2006; Dark Quest Books, 2009; *A Legacy of Stars*, Dark Quest Books, 2012; *The Society for the Preservation of CJ Henderson* edited by Danielle Ackley-McPhail and Greg Schauer, eSpec Books, 2015.

"Sheepdog" by Mike McPhail, *By Other Means* edited by Mike McPhail, Dark Quest Books, 2011.

"Beyond Imagine" by Mike McPhail, *The Stories in Between* edited by Greg Schauer, Fantasist Enterprises, 2010; *Jaelle Her Book*, edited by Melissa Scott and Don Sakers, 2013

"Brothers" by Danielle Ackley-McPhail, *Dogs of War* edited by Mike McPhail, Dark Quest Books, 2013; eSpec Books, 2016.

Contents

The battlefield is an overwhelming place, confusing our senses, shutting down our minds until we hesitate. Sometimes it is but a moment's stutter, sometimes it is forever. Whichever it is, that instant always has consequences. How a soldier recovers is what helps to make them who and what they will become, both on the battlefield and for the rest of their lives.

Greg Schauer

WAYWARD CHILD

Mike McPhail

THE YEAR WAS UC84 BY THE NEW CALENDAR—ULTRA CUNABULAM...BEYOND THE Cradle, as translated from Latin—now, only some eight decades after man first reached for the edge of space, fate gave them the key to trans-light travel. With it, he unlocked the gates to the heavens.

The towering canopy of Demeter's ancient forests cast a perpetual shadow on the ground far below. Against this shadowy landscape, the mind's eye easily imagined yet unseen creatures lying in the nearby darkness; watching and waiting for that one pivotal moment when prey becomes victim.

As the brightness of Tau-Ceti's day turned into the all-consuming black of perpetually moonless night, the monsters of imagination took form; alien to this world, they roamed the darkness in an age-old struggle: survival.

Two of these horrors moved over the root-covered ground with a deft bouncing motion; they negotiated the natural obstacles as if the blinding darkness that encompassed them held no domain. Their appearance brought to mind classic movie images of hellishly huge insects, with smooth carapaces, heads, and protruding mandibles. Their shapes and movements, however, were unmistakably that of man. It became all too clear at the sight of their angular *Maschinengawehr*-style weapons that these were men of war.

"Negative, we ran into another patrol, but managed to break contact," reported Sergeant Bauer, his tone grim; he looked briefly at his helmet's compass display. "We're moving along at one-ten from our initial contact point; with luck we'll swing around them, and then head toward the landing zone," he concluded with a burst of static.

"Acknowledged," replied the disembodied voice; with that the unseen squad leader's icon disappeared from the sergeant's helmet display only to be replaced by the comm's standby marker. As a team leader, Bauer was required to carry an additional signal booster. Tonight he was more than thankful for the surrounding hilly-terrain that played havoc with all but their short-range communications.

Stopping, Bauer half turned to survey the direction from which they had come; in the space of a few heartbeats he was satisfied that there was no sign of pursuit.

Pivoting back, he could see one of his men up ahead. *We're not faceless machines*, thought Bauer at the sight of his fellow trooper; he understood the concept, but never truly felt it himself. Even if his suit wasn't linked to the others via the pacscomp—the suit's integrated computer/squad-level communications—he knew he would still be able to recognize his teammates.

Through his helmet's display a bright green triangular icon topped with MGN was suspended ethereally near the other trooper; he didn't need the electronic identification, to tell this was Morgan. There was just no mistaking the fact that under all that body-armor was a woman; with her wiry-build, she moved more like a dancer than a soldier.

"Maybe that's the problem," he thought, as a wave of anger pushed at him. "Morgan," Bauer called.

Morgan heard Sergeant Bauer call to her over the comm.

"Sir," Morgan replied, still transfixed on the undergrowth, scanning for possible threats. With a snap of her head she briefly looked back toward him; he was double-timing it to catch up. As he closed the distance, he changed step to keep pace with her.

"What was your malfunction back there?" he asked her, getting up close until he practically loomed. His tone was neutral, but his expression shifted with the emotions only discipline kept from coloring his words.

The question gripped Morgan, an unseen force reaching out and engulfing her whole body. It drove the air from her lungs, making it hard to catch her breath. Within a few paces she stopped.

She flashed back to the Legionnaire; through a red haze, she saw the face of the young man. Armed with a bullpup assault rifle mounted with an underslung 30mm grenade launcher, he had been outfitted as a soldier, with ballistic-mesh and plate body-armor. He was no hardened warrior; that had been clear in his nervous and almost confused actions. Most likely a conscript, forced into service in this so-called war. His gaze had held terror as she eyed him over her own weapon's targeting reticle.

With her fingers poised against her weapon's electronic trigger group, she had depressed its safety; like a drumbeat, there was a sudden pounding in her head. She'd tried to concentrate on making the shot, but as she struggled to depress the trigger the pounding threatened to overwhelm her; not until she withdrew her fingers from the trigger guard did the sensation subsided.

"Your inaction..." the sound of Bauer's voice snapped Morgan back to the present, "...put everyone at risk." The sergeant was standing right in front of her; she tipped her head back so that her helmet's side-mounted scopes could look up into his faceless visor.

Memories of her combat instructor, Major Stonebridge, pushed their way into her thoughts. The way he would scream in a put-on, typecast, British drill sergeant voice. "I don't give a damn about your crisis of conscience; when you're out there and some son-of-a-bitch is laying in fire on you and your men..." He would then get up close and personal with one of those standing in the ranks; and in an almost pleasant voice, "...you kill him, and keep killing him. You don't stop killing him until he's a pile of meat." At which point he would rear back and demand that they all shout in the affirmative, then in an almost fatherly way, "After all, do you want to look into the eyes of your comrades, and know, that when the time came...that you...You!" he said pointing off into the ranks. "That you cared more for that son-of-a-bitch..." he paused, "...than you did for them?"

Damnú, she thought to herself in the Irish curse her mother used to use. *I earned my chance to join the squads, and I've already screwed it up.*

After scanning back the way they had come, Bauer turned back to Morgan. "You had him cold. What stopped you from putting a dart through him?" It was more of an accusation than a question.

Fighting back tears, all Morgan wanted to do was beg for Bauer's forgiveness, but that would have put an end to her service in the ADF even faster than her screw up. "I have no excuse." She said as calmly as possible.

The sergeant just stood there for a moment; it was obvious to Morgan that he was considering her answer, and that her future may very well be decided in the next few moments.

With a sharp nod of his head in the direction they were heading, Bauer turned and started to walk, "Get moving, we'll de..." was all he had a chance to say as time slip shifted into slow motion. She felt the shockwave of a fired round and knew there was nothing she could do. Trapped in the moment, Morgan watched as the faceplate on Sergeant Bauer's helmet deformed around the point of penetration. Like a discharging strobe, the world around her disappeared with a brilliant flash of white light followed by intense darkness.

Within moments her vision returned. The return of sound was harsh in her ears as she stared in stunned horror at Bauer's body, collapsed to his knees, and only just starting to tip. The reality of the situation forced its way back into Morgan's consciousness. Stepping back on her left leg, she turned and brought her gauss rifle to the ready position, aiming in the direction where the shot originated. The rifle's targeting reticle hovered about in the ethereal space before her.

She saw nothing; in light-amp mode, her helmet-mounted imaging scopes could pick up enough trace light to turn the darkest night into false-color twilight. Despite that advantage, nothing...no one...was visible.

Her body was in motion before her mind officially gave the order; pivoting on her left foot, she drove herself back toward the massive tree trunk she had passed just moments before. With only a few paces until she reached cover, the air around her became populated by whizzing bits of glowing metal. They flew within inches of her faceplate each leaving a faint afterglow. Momentum took over and finished her bid to reach cover, but not soon enough.

She pressed her left forearm against the tree for stability and closed her eyes to help focus her senses; there was a smack to her right shoulder plate and a violent kick to the side of her helmet. She searched for the hot flow of blood pooling around her neck seal and found none; all she felt was a burning sensation to the side of her head. Static screamed in her ear. It was loud, almost loud enough to drown out the cracks and thumps as more bullets smacked into the tree, ricocheting off the ground around her.

Her heart pounded in her throat as she turned to look. Bauer was on his back, his knees bent and pointing up and away at odd angles; his head had rolled to the left as if looking to Morgan for help. His superimposed identification icon was now red and bordered by a time-stamp, indicating that his suit's pacscomp had declared him dead and beyond reviving. In response, it then fulfilled its priority-one programming and burned itself out, leaving only the recovery signal operational.

"Bauer..." She tried to speak, but her jaw was numb and apparently swollen beyond use; she felt isolated, and with a renewed burst of enemy fire, trapped. Panic pushed at her.

"When shite happens..." screamed Stonebridge out of the past, "...don't stand around mourning your fallen comrades. That is, unless you intend to join them." His face loomed large in her mind, his eyes burning with hatred. "Go and make those sons-of-bitches pay; and pay dearly."

"*Cac,*" Morgan sub-vocalized in Gaelic. "Suit Mode, Slcomm," she said through her inner-monolog; literally reaching out via the nano-scale wires in her brain that formed the lattice work that was the Synaptic Interface antenna.

As always, the suit's pacscomp AI picked up on the standardized keywords she used. "Slcomm engaged," reported the all-too-relaxed voice of the computer. Taking a deep breath, she held it, and then let out a long exhale; it helped—a little. The stress was still there, but now more defined, rather than all-encompassing.

"Brennen from Morgan," she Slcommed, and waited as her pacscomp made contact and communed with her squad leader's. In the span of just a few heartbeats nothing happened; no burst of static over her comhood's headset, no surface thoughts, not even a confirmation icon on her display. Morgan suddenly felt like a small child who had just discovered that her parents were nowhere to be seen.

Pushing back against the growing stress, she tried again. "Bospher Comraden." She thought, using the new open-frequency code words; even if the enemy could intercept this message, they would have no immediate way of knowing its meaning. This from their pseudo-language Ty'Linqua; it meant "Greetings (to my fellow) troopers." In this case, it was a very polite way of calling for help from anyone who could both hear and understand; still nothing.

"Remember the difference between a Trooper and a warrior," she recalled from one of the Major's many lessons. But why this one? It only added to her confusion. Out of her memory, her instructor continued, "You fight as a member of a team, using all the skills and equipment your fellow troopers carry to the fight. A warrior fights alone, relying only on his own abilities and strength of arms."

"What are you trying to tell me?" she thought, "What warning are you...am I giving myself? Yes, I'm alone." That realization almost panicked her, but then she remembered "...fellow troopers and their equipment!" She looked at her team leader, "The signal-booster!"

"Gun, Auto," she Slcommed, and watched as the targeting reticle's quantifier-icon changed, confirming her instructions. Now on automatic, her weapon was capable of putting out some twelve hundred darts per minute—only about a fifth of the weapon's maximum potential—but still fast enough to consume a 90-round magazine in little over four seconds. Her gauss rifle was up and at the ready as she lowered herself to her right knee, its traction pad biting into the ground.

By definition, Morgan was left-handed, but long ago she realized there was very little difference in her abilities with either hand. With a practiced right hand, she reached across her abdomen and withdrew a smoke grenade.

Gripping the beverage-size can against her palm, she depressed the safety bar that ran parallel to its side; a green icon appeared on her helmet's display. Seating her thumb on the arming button on top, she drew back and shifted her body for the throw. She pressed down on the button. Click. The icon changed to red; in an overhand style that any soldier of Earth's wars would have recognized, she lobbed the two-pound cylinder just past the side of her tree, off toward the shooters. Quickly, she stood up and made ready for a second throw.

Some ten yards away the first one landed with a thump, setting off its impact sensor. The grenade deployed three spring-loaded legs that seemingly popped into existence, kicking the cylinder up on end. With a pop, a jet of white spray shot up, filling the air over the canister with a dense plume of slowly falling particles; the cloud ignited, and expanded a hundred-fold in volume.

As the icon changed to confirm the grenade's detonation, Morgan reared back for the long throw, trading accuracy for distance. The second canister arced toward the low-hanging branches, disappearing into the growing smoke screen.

The enemy's base of fire slowed and shifted onto the massive tree she was using for cover; they could no longer see her position, but obviously intended to keep her pinned down.

Now back on her knee and staying as low as possible, she held her rifle with the barrel pointing up and away from what she was doing; she reached out for Bauer. With her eyes fixed on the thermal smoke, she watched as passing projectiles momentarily extruded cone-like shapes from the glowing body of the cloud.

As she touched the all-too-familiar texture of Allied armor, she turned to look; her hand rested on Bauer's shoulder plate, just near his load-carrying harness. Wrapping her fingers around the strap, she tightened her grip and pushed back with her legs. As she worked, weapons fire tore into the side of the tree showering her with fast-moving splinters of bark and bits of hardwood; deflected rounds whooshed overhead.

"Damnú!" she mumbled through numb lips as she hunkered down into her armor, trying to make herself as small as possible; she was more angry than scared. Still kneeling, she released Bauer and grabbed for her weapon's foregrip; twisting herself, she brought the rifle up. The targeting reticle bobbed aimlessly before her, as she tried looking through smoke that for all intents was a visibly impenetrable barrier...or was it?

There! Movement! she thought. It was definitely someone trying to approach her using the smoke screen for cover; but it looked all wrong. It was like a miscolored thermal image: the soldier's face and head were the brightest parts, while everything else faded away through shades of deep red. The background was black with no detail at all, not even reflection from the glow of the target.

Shifting her weapon, she placed the reticle's aiming pip on the target; it failed to lock and just continued bobbing about. "Why can't you see him?" she demanded. "No target designated; range indeterminate." replied the pacscomp.

"Disregard," she thought. "Gun, fixed target," Morgan ordered. The reticle jumped across her display as it switched settings; like iron sights, it was now fixed to a point some three-hundred yards down range along the weapon's line of fire. She swung back on to the target, and with a gentle movement shifted to keep it under her sights.

With a squeeze of her left hand, she depressed the leading edge of the rifle's handgrip; Click. The safety was off and power made available. A pull of the two-fingered trigger would now launch a salvo of electromagnetically accelerated, armor-piercing steel darts.

Time slowed as she waited for the moment to fire; then, in the span of a heartbeat, she looked beyond the aiming pip, and like a rising wind before a storm she felt a growing emotional presence. The bastard Legion soldier, her target. "Noooo! Not this time!" she screamed past her swollen jaw as echoes of the earlier encounter threatened to slow her down. She fought her way past it and tightened her grip.

The world around her erupted in motion as a wave of brilliant white sparks danced across the Legionnaire's chest, dropping him on the spot. Subconsciously, Morgan released the tension on her index and middle fingers; she was up and at a full run before she realized what she had done. The sound of someone screaming pierced the crackle of static in her ears as she ran toward the smoke.

Her scopes went dark as she entered the cloud, but there in the distance—seemingly floating in a void—was another blob of red, another target. Morgan had him under her sights as she cleared the smoke. Through her imaging scopes the soldier was no more than a dark, bush-shaped mass; but to her eyes, the man within the camouflage was clearly visible.

At the last moment the Legionnaire turned toward the sound of her foot falls, but Morgan had him cold. A spray of hot particles was visible through her scopes, overlaid by flashes of white sparks at the points of impact. Beyond the screaming, she heard the crack of the gauss rifle's darts breaking the sound barrier, followed by the concluding thumps of the projectiles punching through mesh body armor, rending flesh and smashing bone.

She continued to run; with her weapon held high and at the ready, she scanned the path with short movements of her head.

In the still air of the deep forest, her second smoke canister created a massive visual void. Its core was almost black through her scopes, only broken by protruding, leaf-covered branches, and partially obscured objects near its growing edges. No one was in sight.

The screaming stopped abruptly, only to be replaced by the whoosh of her suit's air filters opening and closing against her deep breathing. Her throat was raw with the absence of the sound. The front of her comhood just below her lip was wet; not warm like blood, but cool. She was caught in an isolated moment of silence, oddly still amid the rush of combat.

It passed as the enemy renewed their base of fire. To her left an intermittent line of bullets emerged from the void of the cloud as if somehow spontaneously created within; each appearing as a blob of light trailed by its afterglow. The gunner was firing in groups of about five with a short pause in between. The weapon's report was in sync with its passing projectiles; he was very close.

Morgan swung her targeting reticle up and back along the line of fire, looking for the weapon's muzzle flash—or the red of it gunner—but nothing was visible beyond the smoke.

At a burst of enemy fire, Morgan answered in kind; in a sweeping motion she played out a stream of darts toward what she hoped was the gunner's position. Abruptly the fire stopped and the now-familiar red blur of a soldier came into view. Just as quickly the red again shifted into bright white, before fading away.

Morgan was just about to pass into the second cloud when another silhouette appeared. It was the outline of a soldier. He seemed to be sitting, one knee up with his elbow braced against it to support his weapon.

Once again lost in the void, Morgan saw her weapon's pip land on the center mass of the target; with a short burst of fire, a single flash of white exploded on the target, knocking it over.

"Ammunition expended," stated the pacscomp, as the targeting reticle's ordnance counter read triple zero.

"Cac!" exclaimed Morgan as she reached for her ammo pouch. From the handgrip she thumbed the weapon's magazine release; a confirmation icon appeared indicating that the spent magazine had popped free. As she lifted the pouch flap to withdraw a fresh magazine, she approached the edge of the smoke cloud.

Boom! Morgan's reality flinched against the concussive force of the sound combined with the punch of a hypervelocity bullet passing thought the air just inches from her head.

The last Legionnaire she had shot now sat up against a tree just five yards away. Her scopes showed a hot spot on the left side of his chest just below his shoulder. It was slowly expanding. She watched his dark red outline grow brighter as white sparks danced and crackled along his shoulder and over his chest.

His weapon lay in his lap; he pulled back its operating lever, and with a soft ting, the weapon ejected the spent cartridge, which leaped into the air.

Morgan rushed him, not willing to take the chance that she could reload and bring her weapon to bear before he could; the fresh magazine fell from her hand as she grabbed for her weapon's foregrip.

The bloodthirsty screams returned as she fell upon the target, jaw clenched and her thoughts enraged. With the strength of both arms, driven by the mass of her body, she smashed the butt of her rifle into the now-upturned face of the Legionnaire. And again. And again. And…

"Morgan!" said the voice in her head.

She stopped; she was on her knees gripping the weapon's frame around the barrel of her rifle. Beneath her, the body of the Legion sniper lay on its back; its limp arms had obviously tried to protect itself against her mashing blows. The aura was no longer the deep-reds and sparks of white that Morgan had come to expect; shades of dark blue and black instead flooded her vision. Time seemed lost to her.

"Morgan, respond!" ordered the voice.

"Sir?" she mechanically replied via the Slcomm; then she recognized his voice, "Brennen! I mean...Squad Leader." it was hard to focus; it was almost as if being awakened from a deep sleep.

Pushing back, using her rifle for support, she stood up; her mind started to clear.

"Morgan, we're five minutes out..." stated Brennen. With a growing sense of relief Morgan turned to look. There on her display were six green triangular icons. Her relief was short-lived as a red, time-stamped icon appeared. Sergeant Bauer....

"Fall back to Bauer's position and standby. Acknowledge?" instructed Brennen.

"Set." Slcommed Morgan. With the somber realization that the person she had been was no more, she turned and walked back through the gently dissipating smoke. Not just returning to the body of her fallen comrade, but walking toward an uncertain future.

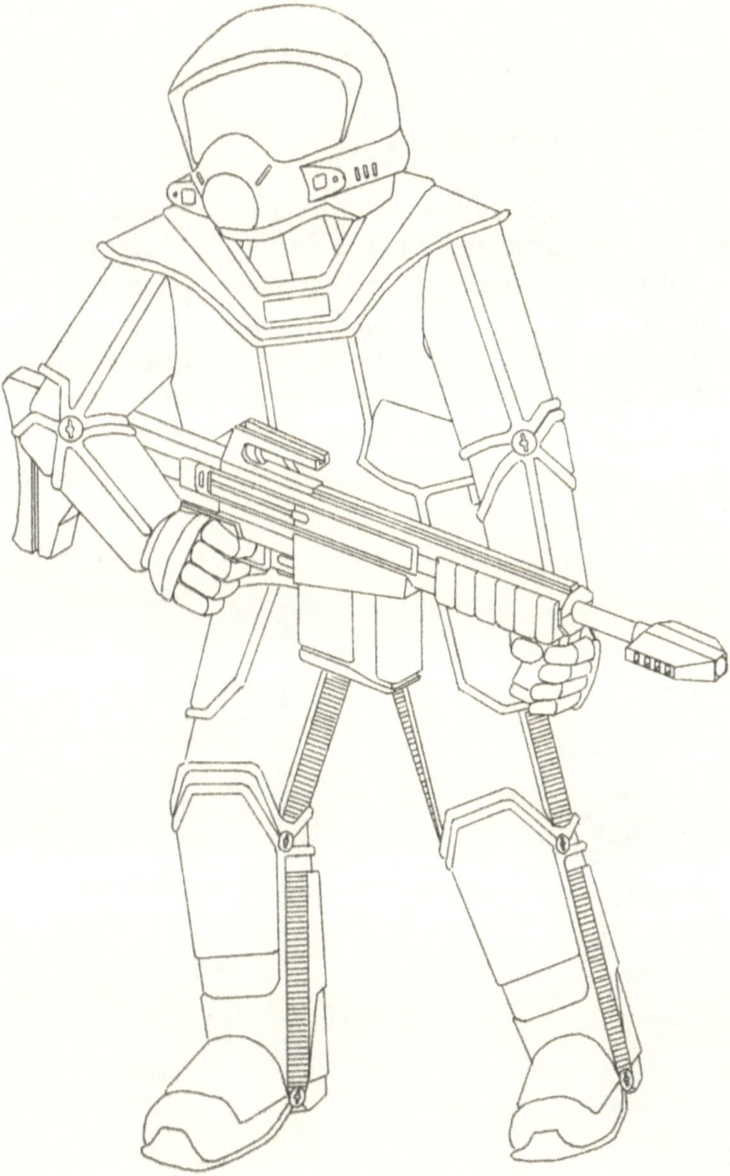

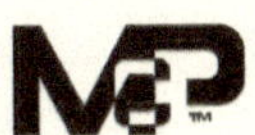

Allied Trooper in Power(ed)-Armor
w/PAC Defender heavy rifle

Concept Drawing

The gauntlet is one of the hardest parts of boot camp, a necessary obstacle to perfect a soldier's training. Running a course while the other cadets that share your barracks attempt to keep you from finishing. The goal is to remain on your feet until after you have crossed that final line, no matter the cost, to you or your attackers. But sometimes what trips you up before the end, comes from a most unexpected place.

Greg Schauer

TURTLES ALL THE WAY DOWN

Danielle Ackley-McPhail

*I*T WAS A TRAINING EXERCISE*. J*UST A TRAINING EXERCISE*.*

Kat had to keep telling herself that.

The telling wasn't a problem.

Remembering? Much harder.

Checking the connectors on her harness and pack and readjusting the lay of her gear, Cadet Katrion Alexander stepped up to the line. Below her was the path down the mountain. At key points, pennants marked off the zones she had to transverse. It seemed clear. It seemed easy. One of the first lessons they'd learned in Basic...never trust how things *seemed.*

"Soldier, is there a problem?" Sergeant Dunn called out behind her, his words snapping hard against her ears.

"Sir, no, sir!"

"Then move your candy ass down that course, now!" his voice climbed higher with each syllable uttered.

"Sir, yes, sir!" Kat screamed as she barreled off the line. She was in full kit, carrying a 70-pound load, with her rifle gripped in both hands, one on the butt and one on the barrel. Her eyes tracked from point to point, assessing any possible ambush. Her objective: reach the bottom on her feet, with all her gear. Her opponents' objective: knock her flat on her back and keep her there. It was called turtling, and with good reason; in full kit, when a soldier ended up on their back the pack lifted them high enough to stranded them like a turtle on its shell.

Not hardly, Kat thought to herself. She set her jaw and moved down the path with steady caution, eyes scanning and rifle at the ready, not for firing, but to use as a . From her left there was a rustle, then a form lunged out of the brush. Kat dropped into a crouch and brought up the butt of her weapon, connecting with the balaclava-shrouded attacker. A blow to the faceless opponent's chest burst the squib in the training harness. The moment the dye was released they dropped back, hands raised, sunlight glinting off their goggles so that even then she had no clue of the vanquished's identity.

Kat didn't care; didn't even bother to watch. She pivoted as soon as she'd confirmed the "kill" and continued down the winding path. Passing the first markers, she moved with care as she skirted boulders and other variables in the terrain. Training kicked in and she kept her pace steady and unrushed, always confirming the space in front of her was sound before she moved into it. Halfway to the next marker she discovered a laser trip-line across the path. She scanned nearby for other traps set to trigger deadfalls along the path engineered to cost her her footing. Taking care she navigated the zone, alert for potential attacks as she did so.

"Come on, soldier! We don't have all day! What, do you think this is a walk in the park?"

The sudden bellow startled Kat, sending her feet skidding in the dust as her load unbalanced. There was laughter from above.

"I think we're gonna have ourselves some snapper soup for chow tonight, gentlemen!"

With a grimace Kat caught herself and heaved back upright, forcing the sounds of the others from her thoughts. Her entire focus was on the course. Another set of pennants flapped as she went by. She was starting to get winded, the downward momentum working against her. It was a struggle to remain upright when both gravity and her kit kept trying to tug her down. But she did it. Because no matter how loud the hecklers got up there, they were no match for the still, soft voice in her head. Cherished and steadying. *You gonna let them get you down, baby-girl?* Kat held on to the memory of her PawPaw's words, often spoken to her when her spirits were flagging and the temptation to give up was strong.

Not. Today.

Growling deep in her throat, Kat ducked as something came at her from the back left. She pivoted and dropped in a controlled squat, kicking out with her right leg. Her ankle was caught in a hard grip. Without having to think about it, Kat brought her rifle butt down, aiming for the wrist holding her tight. Her opponent released and dropped back before she connected, feinting with their own weapon. Before she could recover a heavy weight slammed her from the right. She had to scramble to get her knee braced as she pushed back against the impact.

"Break away, Alexander! You think this is a dance or something? For Crimeny sake! Who cleared you for the corps anyway? Move it! Move it! Move it! We ain't got all day, Cadet."

Distracted, Kat caught one in the chin from an elbow jab...or maybe it was a boot. She was having a hard time telling. Sweat blurred her vision and the double attack had her attention split. In either case her nostrils were filled with the sweet-copper scent of blood. She spat at the assailant on her right, hoping to foul his goggles enough to temporarily get one of them off her back. Literally.

Scrambling, she broke away, lunged forward and found herself in the safe zone; the *thwap* of the canvas pennants sounded more like another taunt. Somehow she was three fourths of the way through...but she wasn't relaxing yet.

Suddenly, behind her, came the thud of booted feet pounding the hard-packed trail. Many booted feet. It wasn't possible to glance back past the bulk of her kit, but Kat didn't need to.

"Aw, shit!" Taking a firm grip on her rifle, she double-timed it down the slope, dodging and praying every step she went. As the incline lessened and her pursuers were still yards back, Kat let a grin slide across her face.

She never should have.

With the next stride her right foot came down on something in the grass, hard and smooth and curved. Her foot slipped and Kat went back, thudding hard across her pack. Her eyes closed and her lungs struggled to draw breath, while her left leg screamed at being bent back almost beneath her. The thud of running feet stopped close by. Inwardly, Kat groaned, then slowly opened her eyes. Sergeant Dunn squatted down next to her, a smirk on his face.

"Shake it off, soldier," he said as he placed something on her chest. "No one makes it down that hill without landin' on their backs at least once.

"Of course...most don't have such professional help being turtled."

Kat shook her head and looked at him in confusion, only to groan again as she looked down at her chest. For a moment, she forgot about figuring out how to get up. She lay there staring into the face of a startled box turtle with a tell-tale scuff across its thick shell.

One thing you can count on in a war is that the enemy will trot out their newest secret weapons. The battlefield is the perfect petri dish to test new technologies. But they don't always work as they were originally intended.

Greg Schauer

CHIMERA

circa 2042

Mike McPhail

TAU CETI THREE—DEMETER—HAD NO NATURAL SATELLITE TO LIGHTEN ITS NIGHTTIME sky, yet to its human colonists, this new world had proven a kindred spirit to their old home. Tonight alien things moved about the old-growth forest; strange creatures that brought with them the ancient need for war.

Ma'Rou stood hidden by the tall wind-blow grass at the edge of the forest and searched the darkness for any sign of intruders lurking nearby. Standing about one foot high at the shoulder, his appearance was that of something man-made, but he moved with a grace and certainty of a born hunter. Clad in contoured armor plating, affixed over a heavy mesh suit, one might assume that he was some soulless machine of war, rather than a creature of flesh and blood. Both descriptions had merit. Ma'Rou was a Parr, a feline by-product of the mind-machine interface experiments conducted by Dr. Jonathan Parr. Equipped with a synaptic interface as a result of those experiments, the Parr had become the covert eyes and ears of the Alliance military.

"Don't go too far up range," psicommed a voice in Scout Ma'Rou's head, *"with your transponder off, it's hard to keep track of you."*

Ma'Rou stopped, casually turning to look back in the direction of his teammates. His display showed three florescent green triangles super-imposed over the landscape, each one had a slightly different internal marking, capped by a three-letter reference code representing the name of its user. The icon MKC was the closest, designating Trooper MacKencey, his handler and friend. The other two icons were further back and proportionally smaller to help denote their relative distance.

"Suit Mode, range to nearest icon," Ma'Rou thought. A mark appeared beside the icon linking it to a line of data; TRP MKC SCT 021. Ma'Rou shifted his attention to the compass displayed at the bottom of his helmet's visor; it read 284 degrees as he lined it up with the icon. After some quick math, *"I'm at twenty-one meters, bearing one-oh-four,"* he thought. In a fraction of a second, the suit's onboard computer interpreted his message and transmitted it via the Psicomm.

"Acknowledged," MacKencey responded. *"Do you have anything?"*

Ma'Rou turned to inspect the grass-filled clearing before answering, *"I thought I had something on the EM scan, but its signal was intermittent."* Then as if on cue, small rhythmic pulses peaked along the green line of the electromagnetic graph. *"Stand by,"* he added. He tried to localize the direction by moving his head from side to side. Suddenly, the EM peaks grew rapidly in strength.

More out of instinct than training, Ma'Rou crouched down as low as possible on all fours and used the grass for cover. With his armored belly touching the ground, he felt the vibration of something approaching fast. His fur puffed up under his armor and the primal part of his mind screamed *Run!* True to his training, though, Ma'Rou held his ground and tried to get a bearing on whatever headed his way.

"MacKencey!" he mentally yelled over the Psicomm. Without waiting for an acknowledgment, he growled, *"Something big."*

That was all he managed before whatever it was ran past him. He tried to get a good look at it, but couldn't. Even through his suit's night-imaging scopes all he saw was a large, dark silhouette moving fast against the background of the night. The sight filled him with primitive terror.

"Ma'Rou, say again," psicommed MacKencey, as he took up a kneeling position next to the trunk of a massive tree. He scanned in the last known direction of the Parr. In light-amp mode, his helmet's imaging scopes picked up and amplified enough ambient light to turn the dark world around him into a pseudo-color day; but still nothing around him looked out of place.

"Troy report," inquired the voice of Sergeant Thompson over the trooper's comm.

"Standby, something may have happened to the Parr," he commed back. Taking a deep breath, he shifted his weapon into the ready position, making sure to keep the targeting reticle in his helmet-display aimed high, for he had no way of knowing Ma'Rou's position.

"Ma'Rou from MacKencey..." the trooper psicommed, straining to hear any response, *"... can you hear me?"*

Unlike the conventional comm system, the Psicomm has no click or beep to announce the beginning or end of a message, and in personal contact all it was supposed to transmit was the voice of the sender, nothing else; but as the message started to form in MacKencey's mind, an overwhelming sense of imminent danger surged through his body.

"It's coming your way!" Ma'Rou screamed into MacKencey's brain, seemingly willing him to get up and run from some unseen horror.

It felt like MacKencey had stuck his finger into a powered light socket. He fought to regain control over his body and suppress the external sense of terror. Disengaging the Psicomm and getting a handle on his emotions would have been the smart thing to do, but that would have left Ma'Rou out there on his own, and that wasn't going to happen. With the sound of his own heart pumping in his ears, MacKencey forced himself to slow down his breathing and get his mind back on the business at hand. He searched the darkness for whatever threat approached.

"Sergeant, Ma'Rou reports that something is moving up on us, but I still have nothing on light-amp," he commed. "Suit mode, thermal imaging," he instructed his suit's Pacscomp. As his display shifted into shades of cool blues and warm reds, something moved into his field of view at the very edge of his peripheral vision.

Just as MacKencey heard the beginning of Sergeant Thompson's response a heavy thump sounded behind him. He pivoted, but before he could react, there was a blur of motion, followed by a hard impact to his head. MacKencey's consciousness swiftly faded out.

"By Jonathan! This is no time to be dead, monkey boy."

A disembodied voice drew MacKencey from the darkness. It spoke with Ma'Rou's all-too-familiar feline tones. MacKencey wasn't too sure he was ready to wake up. It was like falling upward from the bottom of a deep, empty well. One someone had dropped him down in the first place. Everything hurt, but nothing as much as his head. Still, he was awake now and there was no going back. MacKencey groaned as reality slowly came back into focus; no doubt in an effort to bring him around, or at least work out his frustration at his demise.

"Ok...enough, I'm still here," MacKencey groaned at the growling Parr that bounced up and down on his back. A burning pain in his temples flared at the sound of his own voice, "God, I'd hate to be dead and feel like this," he added as the Ma'Rou jumped from his back.

Slowly and with great care, MacKencey moved each part of his body and found everything still pretty much intact. As he sat up, a wave of nausea hit him. He fumbled for the helmet's release claps. Embarrassing as it would be to vomit, it could be fatal if he did so with his helmet still on. He reached up with both hands and attempted to grab hold of his helmet's side-mounted scope housing. He had to get his hands into the finger depressions on top. He felt for the wrap-around traction pad. Once his hands were in place, his thumbs would automatically line up the clasps on the underside of the helmet. Or at least that's how it was supposed to work.

His right hand found its mark; the left one came up empty. The scope was gone. Panic started to well up, increasing the pain in MacKencey's forehead until it practically blinded him.

"Remember your training," he said to himself, practically hearing the voice of his instructor, "Focus on what you need to do to survive." Concentrating, he forced himself to calm down. His breathing slowed. As it did, the pain and nausea slightly lifted. His head still throbbed, and his raw throat burned, but he regained control.

He looked down at Ma'Rou, who now sat in front of him with his head slightly tilted to one side. When MacKencey moved his head from side to side, the image distorted with the motion. He realized that there was something wrong with his helmet's display, the Parr's icon was still visible so there was some functionality left, but the distortion worried him. He hoped that the problem was with the equipment and not him.

"*Can you see anything?*" Ma'Rou psicommed. Without waiting for an answer, the Parr continued, "*Your helmet's torn open in the back and it looks like your Pacscomp's had it, too; the housing's gone and all that's left is the interface connections and one of the high-density antennas.*"

McKencey lowered his hands form his helmet. "If my Pacscomp is gone, then how are we communicating?"

"*Maybe I'm putting out enough energy at this range that your remaining antenna is picking me up?*" psicommed Ma'Rou.

"Not likely," MacKencey stated, still managing to think clearly through the pain. "You still need the Pacscomp to interpret and translate the incoming signals, let alone transfer them to your synaptic interface."

"Well then you have two choices," Ma'Rou responded with amusement in his voice. *"Either you're somehow picking me up on your remaining antenna, or we are communicating directly mind to mind."*

MacKencey's brain ached at the prospect. "Let's go with the antenna pick-up theory, I'm not up to having a religious moment just now."

"Works for me," the Parr psicommed.

Although the pain had started to subside, MacKencey found it hard organize his thoughts. "What happened?" he asked.

A feeling of guilt preceded the Parr's response. *"Whatever it was ran past me on all fours. Its arms and legs were skinny, and kind of reminded me of the way a giraffe moved."*

"A giraffe?" said MacKencey as he started to look around for his weapon.

"If you're looking for your rifle, don't bother. It's in pieces over there." Ma'Rou stood up and pointed with his body.

MacKencey groaned as he saw the state of his weapon. All he had left now was the pistol secured to his hip against an unfriendly armed with God knew what. Then MacKencey's gut suddenly clenched in realization. He turned to look back in the direction of his teammates; no other icons were visible. *"Thompson from MacKencey,"* he commed urgently. No response. *"Williams do you read me?"*

"Save it, Troy," psicommed Ma'Rou, *"After it killed you..."* he paused and walked a few feet off toward where the rest of the team lay, *"...it ambushed the others. Over there at about twenty meters."* MacKencey's gaze followed in the same direction. For a moment, he stared into the distance, jaw tightening at the two time-stamped florescent red icons that now blinked on his display. The feeling of loss was intense.

Ma'Rou turned and walked back to MacKencey, settling again at his feet. *"I confirmed that they were both dead."*

"Damn it," MacKencey said, knowing all too well that now was not the time to mourn his fallen comrades, not unless he planned to join them. Reaching around to his right hip, he released the safety catch that held his sidearm secure inside its form-fitted shell. With a practiced hand, he drew the pistol and brought it up for inspection.

"Where'd the little bastard go?" he asked as he worked the side of his pistol until the weapon was loaded and ready to fire.

"The beastie ran off toward our landing site," Ma'Rou circled in careful, stiff-legged steps. In contrast, the tip of his tail twitched back and forth

in rapid jerks. *"I don't know if it thought there were more of us, or if it was trying to cut off our line of retreat,"* he speculated.

MacKencey held the pistol out in front of him and pointed it at a nearby tree. He then depressed the leading edge of the pistol's handgrip, releasing and cocking the firing pin. A pull of the trigger would now discharge the weapon. It also should have signaled the suit to generate a targeting reticle, which it didn't. "Oh, like I wasn't expecting that," he grumbled to himself.

Ma'Rou turned in response to his statement. *"Trouble?"*

MacKencey rolled onto his knees. "Yeah, my targeting is out," he said as he pressed his free hand into the tree to steady himself. "I'll have to take off my helmet to shoot with any accuracy." The very thought filled him with apprehension. Without his helmet, he would be blind against the night.

"You're in no shape to take this thing on, and with your Pacscomp gone we have no way of contacting the others. We need to get away from here." The Parr headed away from the last known direction of the attacker. He stopped after a few feet and turned back to see if his friend followed.

MacKencey just stood there and leaned against the tree considering his next course of action. It could take hours to climb down to the road, let alone walk into town trying to avoid being detected by the locals. Besides, time was not on his side; in less than an hour the team would be overdue, and with no contact his comrades would deploy another squad to investigate. *They would likely suffer the same fate as we did*, he thought to himself. He couldn't let it come to that.

He pushed off from the tree and took a step toward the Parr. The pain in his head increased with the motion and a persistent ringing sounded in his ears. "No drugs," he said to himself; despite the lovely military pharmacopoeia at his disposal, without the suit's Pacscomp A.I. to make an empirical diagnosis of his injuries, he could very well incapacitate or even kill himself. He couldn't risk an error now. He gritted his teeth and pushed past the pain.

"Scout Ma'Rou," MacKencey said in as firm a military manner as he could.

In response, the Parr turned and sat upright facing him, *"Sir,"* he psicommed.

"What shape was either Sergeant Thompson or Trooper William in?" he asked, not really wanting to know the details, but needing the intel.

A sense of the Parr's dread and horror pushed at MacKencey emotions, *"What that thing did was unimaginable,"* Ma'Rou psicommed as he walked back. *"It literally bent and twisted their extremities until they snapped under the torque; it was as if it was trying to kill the men without damaging the armor."*

MacKencey tried to force the image from his mind and took a deep breath, "Right," he said, then took another deep breath. "Their Pacscomps self-destructed when they died, but Sergeant Thompson carried an external long-range comm; if the beastie didn't mess with it, we have a shot at calling home."

He pointed roughly in the direction that the Parr had indicated earlier. Ma'Rou understood and led the way to their fallen comrades.

Walking over the uneven, root-covered ground would have been tricky under normal conditions. With his head pounding and ears ringing, Mac found it even more difficult, though not impossible. His head throbbed harder with each misstep and stumble.

"Ma'Rou," he said.

"Yes?" replied the Parr

"If that beastie shows up I want you to make a run for it; it's vital someone survive to report this." MacKencey looked around as if just speaking of the creature would summon it.

Concern mixed with stress flavored the Parr's response, *"You know that Chean would never let me back in the house if I left you out here."*

Mac's chest tightened at the mention of his wife, and the worry he'd tried to suppress. "You have my instructions, otherwise this was all for nothing."

"Acknowledged," psicommed Ma'Rou. MacKencey sensed the Parr's nervous tension at the prospect of being out there all alone.

As they approached, MacKencey made out a shape in the low grass. An armored boot rested on a massive root that protruded from the ground. The boot belonged to an Allied trooper.

They were less than five yards away from the body when Ma'Rou stopped, and suddenly tensed, his head pivoting in alert. He turned and looked off to the side, then ran for higher ground. As he leaped up onto a near-by rock, MacKencey's heart almost blew out of his chest at the possibility of his attacker's return. "Report," he demanded.

"Stand by," the Parr murmured, as he moved his head slowly from one side to the other. *"We have company, and it's not the beastie."* MacKencey

moved toward the rock and took up a position behind the Parr. Through his scope, he could make out three pairs of small, infrared spot lights, like the kind found on light-amp goggles. The configuration was not Allied issue. The sight dispelled his fears and helped focus his mind as the unknown intruders were identified as a familiar enemy.

"That makes sense," said MacKencey. He quickly turned and surveyed the surrounding area. "This way," he said then took off at a quick jog.

Ma'Rou jumped from the rock and ran to catch up, *"What makes sense?"* he psicommed; The Parr's question went unanswered as MacKencey jogged on.

The sight of the dead trooper was pretty bad, but in some ways, it didn't live up to the horrors that MacKencey had imaged. The trooper sprawled on his back with his arms flung out to his sides. The leg they'd spied on approach rested atop the protruding tree root, while the other folded back underneath his body at a normally impossible angle. His head tilted back and to one side; the ground around it seemed unnaturally smooth and mirror bright, looking almost like hot tar in the false-color images from MacKencey's night vision scope.

MacKencey just stood there looking down at the trooper and cursed himself. He considered the downed men more than just comrades-in-arms, or even friends—yet without his identification icon, Mac wouldn't have been able to tell this was Sergeant Thompson and not Trooper Williams.

"Troy, hurry up," called the Parr, a sense of urgency and the need for flight underlined his message.

"Acknowledged," MacKencey responded, as he searched for the trooper's weapon. "Where's his gauss rifle?"

"I didn't see it last time I was here," psicommed Ma'Rou. The Parr seemed on the verge of making a run for it. The scout tensed, then dropped low.

"Troy, take cover!" he called out as he started toward a nearby tree.

MacKencey stopped and looked in the direction of the strangers. Through his helmet's directional pickup mic, he heard their approach over the normal night sounds. Crouching, he moved quickly and quietly toward Ma'Rou's position.

Even over the continued ringing in his ears MacKencey heard the men draw near. They were anything but stealthy as they moved through the forest's undergrowth and deadfall. In fact, at least two of them talked aloud, as if they were just taking a late-night walk in the park. In the meantime, Ma'Rou had moved to a vantage point among the tree roots to watch their approach.

"They're over here somewhere," one of them said to his companions. "Chimera indicated that it took down three targets."

"Chimera," thought MacKencey, "a mythological monster, how appropriate."

"Over there!" said another, almost shouting with excitement, "I see a boot sticking up."

In response, MacKencey tightened his grip on the pistol, which he held with both hands at the ready, near the side of his head. "What do we have?" he asked Ma'Rou.

"We have three men in heavy mesh body armor; two are armed with bulky, drum-fed assault weapons; the third is unarmed and holding a data pad." Ma'Rou psicommed.

MacKencey held position as the Parr continued to report. The two armed men moved up, their helmet-mounted, infrared spotlights lighting up the body of the fallen trooper; they kept the body at gun point as they kicked at it. Satisfied that he was either dead or immobilized, they lowered their weapons. They called over the third man. Without waiting, one of the armed men slung his weapon and knelt down next to the trooper.

"Troy, they're searching Sergeant Thompson," he psicommed; hatred underlined his words. MacKencey subvocalized a growl at Ma'Rou's report. He watched as the third man drew closer. Ma'Rou reported that all of them had a dark-colored plastic tag hanging from the front of their armor.

MacKencey's stomach tied itself into a knot. "Ma'Rou can you access the sergeant's base computer?"

"Stand by," the Parr replied. Time clicked by in heartbeats. *"Affirmative."*

"Okay, when I give you the word, activate his helmet's spotlights; full spectrum and at maximum diffusion," he instructed.

"Acknowledged." A strange feeling of both excitement and mischief played down the link between them to echo on MacKencey's emotions. *'I'm never going to get a handle on how the Parr think,'* he admitted to himself.

After sliding his pistol back into its holster, MacKencey carefully reached up and grabbed a hold of his helmet. His right hand gripped the familiar guide points; his left had to probe along the damaged underside to find its mark. After a few moments of searching, his thumb final slipped into the clamps opening. With both thumbs he pressed forward against them. The neck seal gave with a faint snap as it separated from the base of the helmet.

A rush of crisp air slipped past the gap in his suit. The flood of diverse green smells from the forest briefly captured his attention. For a moment, all he wanted to do was sit there and let the cool night ease his burning head and calm his stressed nerves. The sound drew the Parr scout's attention. Ma'Rou turned and watched as he finished removing his helmet, revealing a dark gray, astronaut-style comhood. Two extendable cables still connected his helmet to the armor. Carefully, he lowered it down behind his head on top of the suit's armored backpack, where it promptly locked itself into place.

Blinking hard, MacKencey's eyes went wide, dilating in reaction to the darkness. Drawing his sidearm, he once again brought it up to the ready position next to his head. He knew that the ballistic-mesh body armor the enemy wore was no match for the five-millimeter, armor-piercing spitzers now chambered in his sidearm. Only a strike against a steel or ceramic trauma plate might deflect the projectile. There was satisfaction in that knowledge.

After a few deep breaths, he looked blindly in Ma'Rou's direction; "Ready," he said quietly.

"Ready," psicommed Ma'Rou as he returned his attention back to the strangers.

MacKencey gently shifted his weight from his knees, back onto his feet. He slowly stood up and used the tree for cover. His mind raced as the ancient fight-or-flight response kicked in on a wave of hormones and adrenaline. He suppressed the urge as the world around him shifted into sharp focus and time itself slowed down. "Now," he ordered as he pushed himself around the side of the tree.

Suddenly, the fallen trooper's helmet lights flared. The delicate electronics of the strangers' night-vision goggles overloaded, which set off the failsafe to prevent them from burning out. With the power cut, the enemy soldiers were plunged into a technologically-induced world of darkness.

The men swore, their hands grabbing for their goggles. MacKencey leveled his weapon, squinting against the glare. His training took over as he subconsciously aimed and fired at any potential threat.

In rapid succession, MacKencey fired two rounds into the head of the man standing at Sergeant Thompson's feet. The sound of the impacts rang like a hammer smacking against concrete. Before the body even hit the ground, MacKencey shifted his aim to the second man, who had already raised his goggles and used his forearm to shield his eyes.

Shots echoed through the woods as the first round punched through the soldier's arm and tore through his face. With the dampened recoil of the weapon, the second round landed just above the first, striking him at an upward angle in the forehead. The man's life ended abruptly.

By the time the second body rolled over, MacKencey already had the last man in his sights. Only the terror in his expression prevented MacKencey from firing.

"Don't move!" he yelled as he started toward the man. In response, the soldier opened his hands and spread out his fingers to show he was unarmed; he had dropped the datapad when the first shots were fired.

"Cover me, but stay here," ordered MacKencey to his unseen companion.

"Yes, sir," responded Ma'Rou via his suit's external speakers. The flat, monotone voice was deceptive, to say the least. No one would ever have expected that it belonged to a twenty-pound house cat.

With his pistol held at eye level in a two-handed grip, MacKencey carefully stepped over the body of his fallen comrade. "Okay, you know the drill," he said sarcastically while still moving slowly toward the soldier. "Helmet off; hands on head, fingers interlocking."

The man's hands shook as he slowly undid the chin strap on his helmet and then lifted it from his head.

"Drop it behind you," MacKencey instructed.

The man let it go and put his hands on top of his head, as directed. The helmet gave a muffled thud as it landed. MacKencey stepped up and pushed the muzzle brake of his pistol into the man's neck. Reaching around with his left hand he opened the man's holster and withdrew his pistol, which he threw into the undergrowth behind him.

Ma'Rou reminded him of the plastic tag hanging from the stranger's vest. *"Troy,"* psicommed Ma'Rou, *"I think they're wearing some form of electronic tag."*

MacKencey stepped back and surveyed the stranger; reaching up he grabbed the two-by-four inch piece of black plastic. "What's this? A lift ticket?" he asked, then pulled at the object. It came away with a snap.

"No!" gasped the stranger, his eyes widening in horror.

A sudden, but not unexpected *tick, tick, tick* sounded through the external speakers on Ma'Rou's helmet. MacKencey could picture the corresponding series of small sharp peaks that would have appeared on the electromagnetic grid at the bottom of the Parr's helmet display.

The Parr's horror once again pushed at MacKencey emotions, but this time he expected it. "Acknowledged," he said softly into his comhood's pickup mic before Ma'Rou could Psicomm. "Remember my order," he added. There was a click as the Parr switched from external back to Psicomm, then Ma'Rou reluctantly responded, *"Acknowledged."* He moved off into the high grass to watch.

The stranger could only hear part of the conversation, but it was enough; his eyes went wide with fear.

MacKencey backed toward one of the men he had killed, "Throw me his tag!" the soldier pleaded. He took his hands off his head and started to move forward.

"Don't!" MacKencey growled as he knelt down next to the gunman's body; the soldier stopped, clearly on the verge of panic.

MacKencey eyed the gunman's bulky assault weapon. *"It had better be full of M142s or I'm so boned,"* he thought to himself, as he dropped his pistol and made a grab for the weapon. He had it unslung and had in his hands when he heard the attack.

Just as the soldier turned to make a run for it, the beastie appeared like an animated shadow, seeming to separate itself from the surrounding night. MacKencey watched as an unseen blow struck the stranger. His last screams were forever trapped beneath his smashed larynx and collapsed trachea. Before he could react, a second blow had struck him about the left side of his head. Like a hangman's noose, the force snapped several vertebrae in his neck. Even as Mac raised the weapon, the stranger's body already tumbled over like a rag doll.

The creature just stood there watching. Waiting. Even with the illumination from Thompson's helmet spotlights, the thing was barely visible. Under such circumstances, the mind tends to invent shapes rather than perceive them, and right then MacKencey's imagination worked over time.

So far, the creature hadn't attacked, which strengthened MacKencey's suspicion that the bodies lying around him had been the handlers...and that the plastic tag he now held was some form of electronic identification. The question now was: could the thing *visually* identify friend from foe?

Forcing his eyes down, MacKencey rolled the gunman's weapon onto its side and checked its fire selector. The toggle pointed at a small green x'ed out rectangle. With the press of his thumb he moved the toggle onto a line of red markers. When he looked up his blood ran cold, the beastie had moved closer. The creature now stood less than three meters away. A combination of fear and curiosity ran through Mac now that he could see it.

The thing that had attacked him and killed most of his team was an anthropomorphic machine standing almost two meters tall. The head connected directly to the torso like a fixed turret, with two covered eye-slits that started in the front and ran halfway around both sides. The barrel-like torso was smooth, almost as if it had been cast in one piece, and colored a light-dampening matte gray. Mac eyed the long, slender extremities. They were tapered, strongly resembling heavier versions of conventional medical prosthetics, those designed to mimic but not appear to be living flesh. His head throbbed in reaction, remembering the strength of those limbs.

"Now be a good monster and just stand there while I kill you," MacKencey thought as he shifted his weight to help resist the weapon's recoil. Firing accurately from the hip—even at close range—was risky, but there was no choice. He couldn't take the chance that the beastie had some level of built-in self-preservation. It wouldn't likely attack a handler, but it might very well run away if he leveled a weapon at it.

Despite a seeming lack of eyes, it just stood there watching the downed trooper, like a guard dog awaiting instructions to strike. As MacKencey sized up the problem, he noticed that the beastie was not actually standing still. It slowly shifted its weight back and forth from one leg to another while its hands anxiously fanned opened and closed.

MacKencey's curiosity didn't stop him from depressing and holding down the trigger; in rapid succession three rounds burst from the muzzle of the automatic shotgun. Against the pounding recoil and mechanical action the angle of the weapon climbed, placing the first round into what might have been the beast's abdomen. On contact, the miniature grenade detonated. Its small, shape-charge warhead erupted into a directed jet of superheated gas. In an instant, a tongue of flame vaporized a hole in the outer armor. The surrounding material melted and splattered about in molten droplets.

With a pop and a bright flash the second round found its mark high on the beast's chest; the third passed over its shoulder and detonated somewhere off in the distance. Releasing the trigger, MacKencey watched as the beastie stood there for a moment, wisps of smoke drifting away from the concentric strike points of the grenades. As if suddenly seized by gravity, its torso collapsed downward onto its hips and its arms dragged through the air to land with a smack against the ground.

Standing, MacKencey brought his weapon up to his shoulder and kept it at the ready. Cautiously, he walked toward the toppled machine; it looked dead. *"No, not dead,"* he thought. *"Destroyed."*

MacKencey lowered his weapon and much to his surprise found the Parr standing next to him. *"Can we go home now?"* the feline psicommed, reaching out his front paw to bat the leg of the beast.

The sight of Ma'Rou curiously pawing at the machine as if it was just some new toy he had found in the yard to play with, broke the tension like a hammer blow. MacKencey laughed. "Ok, I'll go call us a ride," he said and started back toward the body of his comrade.

While MacKencey rummaged around in the fallen trooper's side pouch, the Parr climbed up onto the machine's chest to have a better look. Moving up toward the head, he crouched down to nose at something viscose seeping out of a blown seam along the thing's side.

"Troy, you need to see this," Ma'Rou psicommed. Concern and confusion accented the message.

"Acknowledged," he replied, now holding up the long-range comm unit.

MacKencey walked over and knelt down by the Parr. He stared at the dark liquid oozing out onto the ground. He tried to dismiss what he saw as some form of hydraulic fluid, but in the back of his mind a new horror started to form as a familiar scent assaulted his nose.

Reaching over, he touched the dark liquid. It was warm. He could feel through the suit's contact pads that the liquid was thick, almost oily to the touch. To a soldier, it was an all too familiar sensation...blood.

Concept Drawing | M3P™ | ©1988/2017 Mike McPhail

What happens when soldiers, fresh from boot camp and itching to deploy, are crammed into overcrowded barracks and forced to wait? Where does all that energy and aggression go? Who is it directed toward, Let the fun and games begin.

Greg Schauer

FUN AND GAMES

Danielle Ackley-McPhail

BOREDOM SUCKS. REALLY SUCKS!

Cadet Katrion Alexander lay sprawled across her bunk listening to the trash talk from across the aisle. Around her, her fellow trainees played cards or quietly worked on their kits, cleaning and polishing gear that hadn't seen a speck of dirt all week.

Why? The most recent offensive in the ongoing battle for the planet Demeter had begun. The Dominion forces occupying the next continent initiated opening moves against Allied territory. Kat didn't know the details, but the situation must have been serious. Command had put all the active-duty soldiers at the base on heightened alert, including the instructors, and even brought in additional troops from off-planet. They'd pulled just about everyone they could spare off their current assignments and shifted them to patrol duty or some other security task.

The cadets...for now they did a whole lot of nothing except sit around or pull all the shit details that base personnel had been yanked from. They still had daily duties, but no basic training exercises, just morning calisthenics and nothing else for most of the day, barring meals and grunt work, to keep everyone out of mischief. Thanks to the extra forces brought in, all the cadet units—there were several at different stages in their training—had relocated into the one barracks to make room for the extra troops. The cadets weren't to the point of hot-bunking it, but it was a near thing. The close quarters were a harsh reminder of the ongoing unrest.

Every time Kat thought about the situation her stomach went sour. She swallowed reflexively and had to consciously slow her breathing. The base was well within Allied territory, yet the current conflict had the higher-ups jumping. Distance meant little given the advances in modern warfare. *After all, we're close enough for the Allied forces to use the base for a staging area, right? Close enough to effect drone strikes without even leaving the command center.* Kat grimaced. *Forget fly-by-wire, we've graduated to death-by-remote.*

Lately the grunts cycled out of combat grumbled rumors of intel leaks resulting in heavy casualties at the front. Kat had seen some of those injured. Plasma burns were most common, followed by tearing wounds caused by flechette rounds, but the worst were the traumatic amputations, the result of triggered claymore mines. The tension on base escalated each day. Things didn't look good. She fully expected to wake up one almost-morning to find that all non-combat personnel were being evacuated. Or worse, drafted, incomplete training or not.

Sighing, she rolled over, arm draped over her eyes, only to groan under her breath as an argument broke out across the room. The fight only went on a few minutes before someone defused the situation, but the fact that matters reached the point of *needing* to be defused didn't bode well. The underlying strain had them all on a hair trigger.

Kat had a hard time being sympathetic. The cadets' lack of military deportment had her grinding her teeth. This wasn't her first time through Basic. She'd been in the service back on Earth. Thanks to her mother calling in a few favors Kat had been discharged just shy of graduation. In defiance, she immediately joined up with the Alliance and shipped off-planet. Even out here Mother had influence, just not as strong as back home. Being among the raw recruits grated on Kat's nerves. She couldn't deny that. But the freedom to live as an adult was worth it.

The sergeant on duty came through calling lights out. Kat sighed again and willed her muscles to relax as the banks of lights overhead flicked off one by one. In the dark, the bunk to the left of hers squeaked as a body settled into it. So did the one above. She waited for a sound to her right. And waited. None came. Following instinct, Kat slowly shifted onto her back, scooting up on her pillow as if getting comfortable. Her eyes adjusted to the dim moonlight filtering through the narrow windows high up near the ceiling. She scanned the barracks, her vision picking out the soft mounds of bedding-covered cadets against the hard edges of the bunk frames, but no movement. With an effort she reduced her breathing, as if sleep drew her down, then willed her muscles to unwind while remaining alert and ready.

For a long time, nothing happened, yet instinct told her not to relax. She dropped her eyes down to slits so the whites wouldn't betray she was awake. Something moved. Several somethings. Dark against the dark, slowly advancing in methodical stages. Kat tracked them but did not shift as they came to settle at the foot of her bed. Gradually she increased her breathing and readied her muscles to act.

When something pale and recognizably cylindrical passed over her feet she almost laughed. Almost. Too bad for them she was pissed. Could they be any more juvenile? Pulling crap after lights out was not a good idea, especially pulling crap against her. Silently, she lunged forward and lashed out with the blade of her hand in a move she'd learned back on Earth, striking at the darkness to the right of the pale object. At the last minute she pulled the blow, her hand connecting with minimal force. Enough to get her point across and no more. Someone cursed, followed by the sound of cadets scattering. Whatever they'd been passing fell lightly to her bunk. Heavy footsteps pounded the floorboards from beyond the archway separating their side of the barracks from the duty sergeants' private quarters. Kat quickly dropped prone and let her head roll to the side. Moments later someone flipped the lights on. All across the barracks cadets sat up, eyes trained on the sergeant glowering from the doorway.

"Do we have a problem here?" Sergeant Dunn asked, his tone hard and tight as he scanned the barracks. Was it her nerves, or did he pause a moment when he looked at her?

Kat squinted against the sudden brightness from the LED clusters overhead and did her best to look sleepy, while slowly shifting so her blankets covered the roll of toilet paper that had magically appeared on her bunk.

"No, sergeant," she responded along with everyone else.

Dunn's brow dipped as he glared once more around the room before slapping all the light switches at once, instantly plunging the barracks into near total darkness. Letting out a long breath, Kat flopped back against her pillow. Big mistake. The bunks were hard, uncomfortable lumps. Rubbing her spine where it banged against one of the slats, she rolled onto her side and told herself to sleep.

It didn't work.

Ten minutes went by. Then fifteen, when a faint sound of scuffing brought her to full alert. Her eyes popped open to spy a figure creep from beside her bunk and edge toward the one to her right. It wasn't someone she knew. The silhouette was unfamiliar. She did catch a whiff of a nostalgic scent, though. A faint hint of anise. It called back memories of her PawPaw, sitting on his porch in the South Dakota twilight chewing on a stick of his favorite Blackjack gum. Reflexively she breathed in a little deeper.

The guy must have heard her. He pivoted on one knee and Kat found herself staring eye-to-eye with one of the pranksters. Without a doubt, he wasn't from her training unit. Like her, he was a little older than the usual recruit. Besides, even in the dark she would have recognized that wise-ass grin. That reminded her of PawPaw as well.

Softly she growled, but without as much heat as she might have. Just enough to let him know she wasn't an easy mark for whatever trouble he might think about stirring up. Soundlessly, the guy laughed, then slid into his bunk. Her eyes narrowed, Kat snaked a hand down to the foot of the bed and grabbed the roll of toilet paper still lying there. With a sidewise toss she pegged the troublemaker in the head.

This time he didn't bother to hold back his chuckle.

It took Kat a long time to relax before sleep claimed her.

Kat came awake with a deep groan. Sergeant Dunn didn't even wait for dawn. Before the sun tickled the horizon, he strolled through the barracks liberally applying a baseball bat to the inside of a metal trash can. Where he'd gotten either one of them Kat couldn't begin to guess. The clanging reverberated in her pounding head.

In his wake, cadets tumbled from their bunks to stand at attention by their footlockers. Most of them, anyway. Halfway down the far row a panicked squawk rose from a lower bunk as some fresh-faced kid struggled against a cocoon of toilet paper. Kat saw the cadets to either side of him resist the urge to help; they didn't dare to, not yet. Not with the mood Dunn was in. No one was stupid enough to laugh...aloud.

"Is there a problem, cadet?"

"Sir, no, sir!" he responded, still bound tight to his bunk, his face as pale as his bog-roll wrapping.

"You seem to need this more than I do," Dunn barked. He smacked the trash can down next to the bed with a loud clatter and, without freeing the cadet, turned and stalked away, calling over his shoulder, "I want that back before breakfast...*full*, or no one gets chow."

None of the cadets moved until the sergeant disappeared through the door leading out of the barracks. Once he was gone groans rose uniformly.

One person had the bad judgment to give in and laugh. The sound quickly cut off as knuckles met skin. Those closest to the prank victim scrambled to his bunk and tore him free, tossing the mess of paper into the can. It barely filled a couple of inches at the bottom.

Kat identified at least one of the guilty parties. She stomped over to where he stood and smacked him hard upside the shoulder. The amused smirk on his face just pissed her off more. Rather than invite more trouble with the sergeant she pivoted away, scouring their quarters for any garbage. Her stomach grumbled as she dumped her findings in the can. Another inch obscured the bottom, no more, and the barracks were now rubbish-free.

After calisthenics, it took the coordinated efforts of all the cadets and over two hours—not to mention three false finishes—to scrounge up enough trash to satisfy the sergeant, who merely tamped it all down tight each time they presented the full can. Finally, ten minutes before the chow line was set to close, with the base spit-and-polish clean and the can filled to overflowing, Sergeant Dunn declared the terms satisfied. She hoped this would cure her fellow trainees of the urge to pull more tricks.

Forty cadets scrambled for the food lines. There was enough grub for fifteen of them. Somehow, Mr. Wise-Ass ended up with a full tray. Kat didn't even bother. She filled her gut with thoughts of getting even, and not in any way that screwed the rest of the cadets, either.

Kat should have known better. Should have realized things wouldn't end with just one little prank. It was little stuff. Harmless, really, and nothing as grand as the TP mummification that started it all: soap canisters stowed upside down, with the lids loosened; the bottom of garbage bags scored just enough so they tore after the mark hauled them out of the can...annoyances that caused more busy work than anything else. Easy to hide from the sergeant, but with each occurrence Kat's tension increased. She expected at some point one of the raw recruits would give in to their inner dumb kid and escalate things. The newest bunch weren't disciplined enough yet to understand the balance between pranking and pissing off the higher ups.

On edge, Kat left the barracks before dinner. She took her rifle and cleaning kit out into a warm patch of sun. They had an inspection scheduled for that evening. Ever since the pranks started, Sergeant Dunn ground down on them hard, bellowing over the smallest speck of dirt or imagined woolly-booger, assigning extra duty left and right. Kat didn't mind the work—hell, with this much downtime she was looking for shit to do—but no way would she leave an open opportunity for an official reprimand. Not when Dunn seemed to be riding her extra close, like he pegged her for the mastermind or something. Kat's lips thinned as she considered the ramifications of that. It had been hard enough getting to where she was against her mother's objections. She knew to keep her place she had to stay above reproach because even out here enough people owed Mother favors that several officers on the base had their eyes open for reasons to send her packing.

Going home in disgrace was not an option. Not if she ever wanted to make an adult decision for herself again. Kat reapplied herself to cleaning her rifle, and everything else, until not a smudge or particle remained in evidence, then carefully stowed the weapon, regulation-precise. As she bent over the case, motion from across the way caught her eye. By the barracks, where those who cared to spend their vice credits smoking a cigarette or two, when they could get them. One of the privates that worked in Commander Richtman's office stopped near the ash can. His stance held a subtle tension that made Kat think wistfully of home...or rather, her PawPaw's ranch. Back when she was a girl they'd rescued a wild mustang some fool had half ruined trying to break it. That horse stood the same way when anyone came near the paddock or the pasture. Faking an easy, relaxed stance, but ready to lash out at whoever came too close.

Kat almost laughed as her memory of that mustang chawing prairie grass superimposed itself over the soldier across the way. Not wanting to explain, she restrained herself. The private didn't seem to notice her as he reached into his pocket and pulled something out. Assuming he was there to burn one, Kat went back to putting away her gear.

Once she'd gathered everything, she stood and faced the barracks. She frowned and looked around. The scent of burning tobacco was absent from the air and the guy had already cleared out. He must have decided against a smoke. Or maybe he didn't have enough credits left to get a cigarette out of the military-issue dispenser next to the smoking area. She put him from her thoughts and glanced at her watch. Time to put her shit away and head for dinner. As she walked past the ash can Kat noticed a faint scent of gun powder. She brought her shoulder toward her nose. She couldn't quite say, but that might be her.

Must have gotten some residue on me, she thought. *Great.* She'd have to change before going to the Mess Hall or the smell would put her off her food.

When she slipped inside the barracks to put away her gear and grab a fresh set of BDUs, Kat discovered rows and rows of neatly made bunks, dully gleaming footlockers, and absolute silence. For once there wasn't a cadet in sight...or even a sergeant. Tempted by the luxury of a private shower, Kat took ten minutes to wash the stink off of her. She'd just secured her boots when Sergeant Dunn passed through to his side of the barracks. He looked annoyed to see her. Of course, since being relegated to glorified babysitter he looked annoyed any time he saw any cadet. His gaze sharpened and he looked around, as if searching for a prank to pin on her. The suspicion rankled, but Kat kept her expression neutral. Before she could scramble to her feet, he barked, "Save it, Alexander. Shouldn't you be at Mess right now?" He walked away without waiting for an answer, leaving an air of mistrust in his wake.

That cut it. She'd done nothing to earn his judgment. God help the next person to pull a practical joke. Kat grabbed her cap and headed for the Mess Hall. The base seemed deserted as she passed through. *They must be serving something good for chow today,* she thought. She didn't bother picking up her pace. By now little but scraps would be left, given everyone else seemed to have headed for dinner before her.

Halfway across the compound she forgot all about food. A *whoosh* sounded behind her, and a man cried out. Kat spun, looking for the source of the outcry. Her mouth dropped open and her eyes widened. The barracks. Deep, black smoke shrouded the whole front facing, not quite masking a hunched figure in the midst of cloud. As it quickly dissipated Kat noticed black streaks marked the walls. Smoke still poured from the broken rim of the ash can. She barely paid attention to any of that, though. Her gaze fixed on Sergeant Dunn, crouched against the wall, face turned in.

"Oh...shit..." She vaguely noticed a growing commotion behind her as the Mess Hall, and every other building nearby, disgorged its occupants. How she wished she were among those people boiling into the compound still trying to figure out what happened. Kat knew. She could kick herself for not cluing in to the signs earlier. It never even occurred to her the cadets might not be responsible for all the pranks. This one went beyond good taste, though...and here she stood, frozen in place, looking like the prime suspect.

The same thing apparently occurred to Dunn. He straightened and pushed off from the wall leaving a dingy silhouette limned with dark grey where he'd gone to ground. His gaze never left hers as he stalked toward her.

"Crap!" she swore with more vehemence beneath her breath.

The acrid stench of burnt gunpowder and singed hair preceded him, his craggy face—skin red and tight beneath a veil of loose ash—contorted in preparation for a whole other kind of explosion. Dunn stopped when they were toe to toe. Behind Kat the commotion had stopped as well.

Only extreme willpower kept her from recoiling. From the smell. The situation. Dunn's expression. She never realized exactly how strong-willed she was until that very moment. She felt herself pale, however, as Dunn slowly lowered his face down into hers. He hadn't ducked quickly enough, apparently. His eyebrows were singed and small blisters formed along the edge of his jaw. Kat had the overwhelming urge to close her eyes against the sight. She resisted. Trying not to flinch, she locked her gaze on a thin trickle of blood snaking its way down his face from a cut on his forehead. He must have been tagged by a fragment from the ash can.

"Alexander," he said, his voice disturbingly low. "Do you have an explanation for what just happened?" The compulsion to turn and look for the guy from earlier tugged at her hard, but again she resisted. Dunn growled faintly, reminding Kat he expected an answer.

"Sir, no, sir." And that wasn't a lie. She could guess, but guesses weren't fact. It wasn't smart for a cadet to imply anything about a sworn-in soldier without incontrovertible proof. That kind of thing was bad for a career.

"So, let me understand...you're saying you have no idea how gunpowder ended up in the ash can?" His expression tightened and his right eye twitched.

"Sir, yes, sir," she answered. Her voice came out strained as she braced for his response.

The crowd at her back began to murmur amongst themselves. Kat ignored them, maintaining eye contact with Dunn. His breath came in short, sharp huffs as he searched her gaze. Kat remembered his suspicious looks from earlier and her gut landed in her boots. There was no hope of him believing she had nothing to do with this. She vowed to kick that private's ass the next time she saw him.

After a long moment, Dunn grimaced and stepped back. Clearly, he wanted to scream and yell and tear her a new one, but he couldn't. Not on speculation. Until he had proof she had something to do with it, all he could do...well, all he *could* do was make her life a living hell, but none of that came with a black mark on her record. Yet.

Dunn turned to face the gathered crowd of mostly cadets his gaze sweeping the lot of them before he spoke. "What is this, summer camp? You cad-idiots need to be worn out to keep you out of trouble?"

No one spoke.

Somehow his face turned even brighter red. "Do you think this is fun and games? This is the military. The base is on heightened alert. Start actin' like soldiers, godamnit!" Dunn said, his eyes coming back to pin Kat where she stood. "Whoever's responsible for 86ing the ash can has fifteen minutes to report to the commander's office... The rest of you, you have twenty minutes to prep for maneuvers and get your asses to the parade ground, *someone* just earned you *all* some survival training." The volume of his voice increased with each word.

Everyone held their groans until Dunn pivoted and stalked away in the direction of the medical building. Once he was out of sight Kat turned and glared at those behind her, searching for the dumb fuck that started it all. It disturbed her to see most of the onlookers glaring back.

That faint screaming sound? Her career as it shriveled up and died.

With a scowl, she headed back to the barracks to pack up her kit.

In the end, the sergeants' divided the cadets into four-man teams, mixed so that no one group benefited from more extensive training than the others, and everyone lost the edge of any team cohesion they'd already built up through existing associations. Kat found herself paired with the wise-ass—known more conventionally as Cadet Jackson Daniels—and two others she knew only loosely through duty assignments.

When they'd arrived at the parade ground they were ordered to unpack their kits.

A bad sign.

The sergeants came around and stripped their gear of everything but the basics: rations and hydration pack enough for three days, first aid kit, a knife, and a roll of duct tape. Beyond their personal gear, they received one field comm per team. Night set in by the time the sergeants completed the sort. None of the cadets grumbled but their expressions grew more and more grim, brows lowered and lips pressed thin, hands fisted at their sides. At this point, Kat would have to guard against a blanket party for a good long time.

"Each of you may select a single item from your remaining supplies," one of the sergeants called out, his voice raised sufficient to be heard by all.

"Anyone trying to pick more than one item will have that privilege revoked for their team. I suggest you all choose wisely."

That set off a mad scramble.

Kat watched as her teammates made their selections. Daniels immediately reached for a high-end compass from the top of his discards. It looked like the Swiss Army knife of its kind, certainly not standard issue. The other two cadets selected a pack of flares and a coil of rope. The flares weren't a bad choice, but the rope? It wasn't like they were going to be doing much vertical climbing, and the duct tape was more practical for securing things. Kat started to recommend the other cadet choose the trench shovel also visible in his pile but one look at the glare he sent her way had her raising her hands and turning toward her own pile.

A grimace crept over her face as she considered her choices. There were at least four things she itched to reach for now that she knew what her teammates had selected. The smoke grenades could come in handy, or perhaps the water-purification tablets. In the end though, Kat chose her rifle, a gauss loaded with a full clip and a spare mated to the grip. The tension in her gut told her it was the right choice. None of the sergeants objected as she slid the weapon across her back. Thanks to her previous training she was already weapons certified.

Once everyone made their choices the cadets shoved all the items winnowed out into individual sacks the sergeants provided and scrawled their names across each one in marker on tape. Presumably someone would gather them and return everything to the barracks. When that was done, the cadets stood in silence staring at their miniscule piles. Some of them looked hyped and ready, others looked pissed. No one knew what to expect. Heads came up as, out of the dark, Dunn stalked into sight. Surgical cement held his cut closed and the rest of his face glistened beneath a protective burn ointment. His eyes held a look of pure malice.

"You wanted fun and games? Well you got it. You will repack your gear and head in formation over to the airfield. The waiting helos will take you to the remote training zone." He smirked. "You have four days to find your way back to base."

Someone groaned.

"Have *fun*, kiddies." Dunn turned and swaggered away, leaving the other sergeants to supervise the departure.

As a group, the cadets watched in silence until he disappeared into the night. When he was gone, Kat caught bits of a conversation behind her that snagged her attention.

"They're being kind of hard on them, aren't they?" one of the sergeants said to the other. They talked low, but Kat could just make out what they said if she focused hard.

"Naw, they woulda done this anyway. This just moved things up. Some important intel went missing today during all the excitement. Until they figure out what's goin' on, Command wants to get the greenies out of the way in case the shit goes flyin'."

Anger built in her gut at what she'd just overhead.

"Hey...Kittie," Daniels called from the crush of cadets organizing their packs, distracting her. "You coming with the rest of us, or not?" She looked his way and noticed he held up her empty rucksack. Kat growled. She visualized the many ways she'd like to maim Daniels. Nearly as many as the different motivations he gave her to do so.

"The name is *Kat*," she snapped as she shoved past him to reach her gear, snatching the bag from his hand.

He just chuckled as she went by. Kat's jaw clenched but she said nothing, not wanting to draw any more attention her way. She had too many dirty looks darted toward her as it was. It took effort to ignore them as she repacked and moved into formation, but she managed. Daniels ended up beside her. She ignored him too.

That was significantly more difficult.

The column headed to the airfield at a steady march. Five transport helicopters stood ready and waiting on the tarmac. As everyone started climbing on board Kat lagged behind, not comfortable with having any of her fellow cadets at her back at the moment.

Only the *whump* of the rotors powering up and the bustle of cadets boarding the helos broke the silence. And Daniel's persistent chatter. Kat stood there with her pack in her arms trying to ignore the wise-ass who remained next to her.

"They call me Scotch."

She couldn't resist. "I see," she said, her tone dry as her own inner wise-ass came out to join the party. "That would be because you drive everyone to drink, right?"

He grinned. Kat just stared back, her expression neutral.

"Nah, my drill sergeant didn't know the difference between Scotch and good, ol' Tennessee Whiskey." She must have seemed confused because he laughed. "Jackson Daniels...*Jack Daniels*..." Kat scowled, still not getting it and frankly not understanding why she still paid attention to him.

"You're not much of a drinker, are you?"

At that, Kat gave him a sour look. "Not yet."

This time he laughed loud enough one of the sergeants glared over at them.

"You'll do, Kittie," Scotch said with satisfaction twinkling in his eyes.

Kat pointedly turned away to stare off at the support personnel running last-minute checks on other aircraft preparing for flight. The airfield was packed. To her left, a troop transport went through final check and several wings of PlasmaHawks looked ready for takeoff. Lined up on the tarmac beyond them she counted about a dozen aerial drones, their payloads already secured, engines powering up. Kat's chest tightened at the thought of the wounded that would soon come back. And the casualties that wouldn't.

A frown puckered her brow at the thought and the surface of her skin prickled. She narrowed her gaze and, without realizing it, started walking toward the combat craft. Something about the way one of the men moved set her instincts screaming. The way his eyes subtly scanned the zone as he walked across the tarmac. The casual edging of his hand toward his pocket.

Kat gasped as a recent memory flickered to the surface. It was *him*. The asshole private from earlier, she'd swear it. Only she'd seen him at work in the commander's office on more than one occasion, so what was he doing in a mechanic's overall, shoulders deep inside a maintenance panel on the exterior of a troop transport? Unbidden, Kat took a step toward him as her head tilted, trying to get a better look at what he was doing to the innards of the plane. A growl rumbled her chest. She thought about when she'd first saw this man: the underlying tension, the supposed prank, then just now finding out someone had used the incident as a diversion. Again, he made her think of her PawPaw's mustang. They'd eventually had to put the horse down when a hand got too close and the horse caved in his head with a double kick of his back hooves. They hadn't heeded the warning signs back then; now, Kat had more than learned the lesson. Prank, or something more insidious? Either way, she couldn't stand by without confirming.

"Sergeant!" she called out, not taking her eyes off the private. At the sound of her cry his shoulders tensed and his far hand reached across his waist, as if going for something. Kat's guess was a weapon. She dropped her pack and knelt, positioning herself below the point he would expect her to be, her hand already drawing her rifle around from where it lay across her back. Even if this hadn't been her second pass through Basic, if Kat knew anything, it was guns. PawPaw had made sure of that. She braced on her knee and trained the weapon on the man before her. "Don't move!"

All around her, Kat's words echoed from other throats, followed by the sound of weapons carking. She didn't have time to see where they were aimed, though she suspected at least half of them were on her.

"Alexander, what the hell do you think you're doing?" From the corner of her eye Kat spied Dunn stomping from the hanger and across the tarmac. He appeared beyond pissed.

"It's him, sir, the one responsible for this afternoon's incident."

Across the way, the private's expression twisted into lines of determination and hatred. Kat got a bad feeling as his fist clenched, as if he had depressed a button or something. Then he lunged away from the aircraft, drawing a Dominion-issue Predator 9mm pistol. Kat sighted, stilled her breath, and calmly squeezed the trigger before he could bring his weapon to bear.

Something inside the airplane exploded. Whether in reaction to her shot, or to the explosion, the soldiers around her began to fire. Kat ducked, when from out of nowhere a freight train took her to the ground, rolling protectively overtop of her as it did so. The smell of cordite and burning plastics billowed around them as military personnel scrambled to contain the situation.

"Hey, Sarge. Looks like you were wrong..."

Dazed, Kat stared up at Scotch, her breath still coming heavy as her heart raced, incredulous at his audacity. He really did remind her of her PawPaw. She hadn't yet decided if that was a good thing.

"*What*?" Dunn bellowed. His face deepened to a dark red and a twitch started right under his eye as he closed on where they sprawled, Daniels crushing Kat beneath him. She couldn't complain. He'd likely saved her from a hail of bullets and other flying debris.

"It is all fun and games..." Scotch flashed Kat that wise-ass grin as he motioned toward the body across the way, the face a bloody pulp on the right side where Kat's round had blown out the ocular cavity. "...until someone loses an eye, anyway."

Working on a skeleton crew, ferrying a damaged starship home, can be fraught with tension and personality conflicts. Routine becomes master and monotony king. Then, cutting through the boredom come the unexpected. Whether the source is a practical joke or a ghost in the machine, it is the gremlins in our lives that keep things interesting.

Greg Schauer

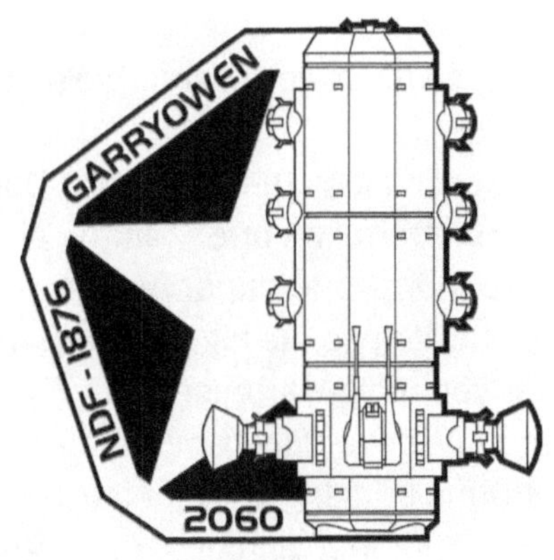

CLING PEACHES

Mike McPhail

"The truth is what you make of it." William Kriegherren

THE YEAR WAS UC104—2065 A.D. BY THE TERRESTRIAL CALENDAR—THE SCOUT Frigate *Garryowen*, NDF-1867, was inbound for the AeroCom Squadron Base, *Brooklyn Yards,* Heartland/Luna America. Damaged by a ground-launched Firemoth missile during the opening phases of the invasion of Demeter, she was running with only a skeleton crew, tasked with ferrying her home for repairs. Now some four-plus hours out from the planet, their next challenge rapidly approached: Transition to hyperspace.

Floating through the last set of opposing hatches, acting Chief Engineer William Donovich entered the drive section's service module. *"By any other name, it's still engineering,"* he thought. *"A magical land traditionally ruled by mad Scotsmen and techno-fetish women."* The very thought brought a smile to his face.

In truth, it was his love of science fiction that had drawn him to study engineering; he always seemed to have a need to find the facts behind the fiction. Eventually, this led him to apply to the National Space Agency where, after months of evaluations, he was rejected on the grounds that he was physically unfit to be an astronaut; whereas the AeroCom recruiter welcomed him with open arms.

Despite the mundane crap of life in the service—and the occasional megalomania of its civilian overseers—there were moments like this; when his daydreams of crewing an all-powerful starship across interstellar space came true.

"It's just a shame it doesn't look the part," said Donovich, looking down from the main hatchway platform; he often felt the ship's SM was less of a grand starship's engine room—one capable of governing the drive field generators that boosted the ship to the higher energy plane of hyperspace— and more akin to a padded, cold-war missile silo, with its lack of interior walls to divide its circular decks into compartments; this in addition to having equipment platforms bridging parts of its central gangway.

Looking back, Donovich could visualize the platforms being lowered through the central hatchways along the gangway's cargo rails, then locked into place and connected to a myriad of pipes and cables by engineering specialists wearing orange MAC suits just like him.

"Wow," he said, a feeling of excitement washing over him. "Now the fun begins." He maneuvered himself to the platform's hatch control station. With a practiced push and heel snap, he locked his foot into one of the station's boot-docks; he activated the controls, which came to life with a myriad of color-coded icons. Looking up, he could see the hatchways, their passage indicator lights both showing steady-green.

"Why can't real life come with its own sound track?" he asked, thinking back and failing to come up with any score or song he could run through his head that would be appropriate to the moment. "I'll just have to wing it," he concluded.

With a quick look down, he placed his gloved finger between the protective side loops of the "Lock All" sequence button. With a gentle press and a confirming click, his world became filled with pulsating yellow lights and the chirp of alert tones.

With the ten-second time count for hatch closure running through his mind, Donovich once again looked up. "The CM's connected to the pod-bay..." he started singing as the first hatch swung into place, to be shortly joined by its pod-bay counterpart, "...the pod-bay's connected to the SM...," he continued as the hatches just above his head swung one by one into place, with a steadfast motion and an accompanying mechanical *whirr*, the SM's main two-meter access hatch pressed into its frame and locked. Its pulsating, yellow warning lights then switched to a steady red.

After checking the status display on the consoles, he looked over the platform and down the length of the SM, "...the SM's connected to the DS; the DS contains the TL Drive, the reactor, and some other stuff." He paused before concluding with a boom in his voice, "OH HEAR...THE WORD...OF THE LORD!"

"Nice little tune," said a familiar female voice.

Donovich turned to see who had intruded on his moment. There was no one. "Duh," he whispered to himself. "Sorry, ma'am," he said into his comm-hood's pickup mics, "I was just running through the hatch checklist." He felt foolish at being caught acting so cavalier about doing his job.

"That's alright, Chief, I'm glad you're not stressing about the situation," reassured Major Ware, the ship's CO. "So I take it to mean that the drive section is secured?" she asked.

"Yes, ma'am," replied Donovich, as he snapped his foot free from the restraint. "I'll just need a moment to get into my station."

"Understood, Chief. Ware out."

With a tap on his arm control pad, Donovich switched his primary comm channel to standby and then opened the squad-band. "Patterson," he called, as he pushed off toward the ramp at the side of the platform; grabbing the handrails with both hands he redirected his momentum down the ramp.

"Patterson here, go'head, Chief," replied a voice with a slight southern drawl.

Donovich passed quickly over the life-boat deck and was now holding on to the top of the handrail loops for the ladder well. "What's your status?" he asked as he looked down through the two stories of wire mesh tubing that surrounded the access ladder.

"Everythin's green, Chief; we're good to go."

"Understood," replied Donovich, while still debating his next course of action. "Go strap in; I'll give the All-Go as soon as I hit my station and get some coffee." With that he pulled himself head-first down the ladder-well; an experience that is visually not unlike diving into a cheese grater.

"Yes'ir," then there was a pause, "Um, did ya'll say coffee?" asked Patterson.

Donovich waited until he had cleared the ladder before answering; free-falling down a ladder-well was just something no sane Starman should do, so getting stuck and having to explain himself as someone came to fished him out was definitely on the top of his "things-not-to-do" list. Now over the main deck, he maneuvered to his station. "Do you remember that guy Tony from the *Vandenberg*?"

"Yeah, I think so; but there were a lot of techs floatin' around, tryin' to glue us back together for the jump home," he remarked.

Grabbing the handhold next to his station's jump-seat, Donovich pulled himself into place below the rack holding his MAC's pressure helmet and its adjoined environmental chest pack. With a snap, he locked his heels into the boot-docks, and reached for the five-point harness handles. "Well, while we were talking, I mentioned that fluid-loading didn't work to keep down the nausea during Transition."

The feeling of the seat's restraining straps snuggling up, and then locking down, was always comforting, and in its own way sort of creepy. "So, he recommended a hot cup of strong coffee instead of that citrus-flavored electrolyte stuff," he continued as he reached for the self-heating pressure-mug. "I love a ship with cup holders," he added as he pulled the mug free from its mount below the console. Depressing the top, he took a long, hard draw from the mug's mouth piece; a satisfying warmth spread through his chest.

"I take it ya'll still got your bag with'n arms reach?" asked Patterson.

Locking the mug back down, Donovich opened the top pocket of his suit's utility jumper and pulled up the open end of a red biohazard bag. "Aye," he confirmed. "Okay, Patterson, I'm about to give the flight deck the All-Go, you set?"

"Yes'ir."

"Understood, Donovich out." A beep signaled that the channel was now on standby. Looking up he could see the underside of his suit's pressure helmet. "Regs state that I have to wear it..." he said doubtfully, "...but after last time...Nope," he concluded and turned his attention to his station's console. All status lights were green, except for the few that were blacked out from the missile strike. He depressed the "All-Go" button and waited for the flight crew to do their part; on this trip that would be just Major Ware and the XO, Lieutenant Koenig.

The two-minute warning klaxon sounded. "Attention all personnel, prepare for Transition," announced the ship's computer over the intercom. It was clear the CO was just waiting for his signal.

Hyperspace Transition Syndrome, or hypes, was comparable to the space-sickness many astronauts suffered as they adapted to living in zero-g. The professionals didn't really know what caused hypes, or who was likely to be susceptible to it—let alone how to cure or even minimize the effects; all Chief Donovich knew was it specifically didn't like him.

Eyeing his console, he wasn't so much monitoring the systems read-outs, as watching for flashing yellow or red icons: once the trans-light drive sequence was engaged, only a full-blown "Blow the main power couplings and pop the compositors," abort could stop it from firing. Even then, it could only be interrupted up until the drive field started to form; after that, you were going for a ride.

Suddenly, the sound of crackling static seemed to come from everywhere, and he could feel the hairs on his body trying to stand up under the constrictive force of his MAC suit. On his console the guard covering the lighted red "Abort" button popped open with an accompanying alert tone. As the saying went, "His ass snapped shut" at the very thought of ever being in a situation where hitting that button was his only option. The pretty, candy-like button was just part of the "pilot factor," where the guy in charge (or in this case, the Chief engineer) must retain some ability to override the computer in the event of an emergency...

Donovich's thoughts were cut short as the drive field formed.

It was said that how one perceived the sensation of entering hyperspace was directly proportional to how often, and how severely, one suffered from hypes. Some said it was like standing on a commuter rail platform in winter as a train speeds by. Personally, Donovich pictured it as falling down a long-forgotten mine shaft somewhere in the frozen hell of Siberia, this after having been drunk for the weekend and dealing badly with a massive hangover.

The actual Transition to hyperspace wasn't the problem; that happened faster than the human mind could ever hope to perceive. All the vertigo-inducing special effects were actually caused by the ship's own TLD systems. It was only after the ship had passed through the point of Transition that the field compensators could finally even out the power flow and balance the drive's harmonics against the resident frequency of the ship's spaceframe.

"Enough technobabble..." he said to himself through clenched teeth, "...knowing doesn't help. Believe me!" The nausea was there and starting to push at him; he reached for the bag's grab tab at his pocket. A heavy thump sounded from somewhere overhead, quickly followed by a sharp metallic ping from somewhere nearby. Donovich looked up. His eyes were tearing; he attempted to wipe them with the back of his glove. "No good," he murmured, and then looked over at his console; no flashing red indicators to greet him. Turning back, he listened for the sounds of escaping gas or grinding metal; there was nothing.

As his vision cleared, he could see that the mission clock had started. It read 482 hours and 56 minutes as the seconds counted down. "That's almost three weeks under driver," he said, now realizing that it was over and that, for the first time, he hadn't lost it all over himself from the hypes.

"Attention all personnel, secure from Transition," sang out over the intercom in the lovely, neutral female voice that was the SC; it was accompanied by the usual low-gravity warning.

Uncoupling his harness, Donovich stepped out onto the deck; now under pseudo .3-g—one of the unforeseen side effects of the TLD was that it creates something akin to its own gravity well—he felt heavy again, with that all-too-familiar draining feeling as fluids once again moved toward their lowest points.

After a few deep breaths and a bit of stretching against the elastic action of his MAC suit, Donovich turned and reached past his console for his pressure mug. He heard the warning tone from the console as his hand touched the mug's handle; in that instant, the very reality around him rapidly compressed and expanded like an image in a carnival mirror.

He grabbed for his jump seat and managed to get a handhold on the frame. The vertigo drove him to his knees, retching, unable to breathe from the abdominal contractions. His other arm was locked straight, with the hand pressed down into the deck in an effort to support himself.

At that moment, he was alone; trapped in the darkness behind his own eyes, with the feeling of being squeezed to the point of suffocation. Then somewhere at the edge of his consciousness he could once again hear the alert tones, now joined by the voice of Major Ware.

Donovich opened his eyes, but growing pressure against his face threatened to force them shut. Somehow, he managed a gulp of air, which he forced down past the burnt feeling in his throat; he hadn't voided his stomach, but definitely refluxed up into his mouth, then he was breathing again.

"Chief, what is your status!" the Major demanded. "Patterson get up there and see what you can do!" she ordered.

"Donovich here," he said with a raspy voice.

"Thank God." There was stress-tainted relief in her voice. "Chief, the SC reports that we've gone into field imbalance."

"Understood, ma'am, I'm on it," Donovich responded, as he scanned along the length of his console.

"I'm headin' up," replied Patterson.

"Patterson stay put..." Donovich countermanded as he pulled himself up to his console on unsteady legs, "...in case the problem's at your end of the module."

"Yes'ir."

Donovich was having trouble seeing—no doubt he'd blown some blood vessels from the strain. It wasn't so much that his vision was blurry, but that every lit display now had a superimposed twin. The console was awash in flashing yellow status lights, each indicating some irregularity with its respective system. They could all wait: red priority markers strobed around the icon for the Drive Frequency Controller. With a touch of the icon, Donovich opened a dialog window stating, "MANUAL OVERRIDE AT DFC UNIT," accompanied by two columns of numbers; one number set was flashing red.

"Damnit!" he exclaimed, looking over at the machinery mounted to the nearby equipment platform. "That's where that bang came from," he muttered, remembering the sounds he heard during Transition.

Like a chimp climbing slowly through the treetops, Donovich reached out from one handhold to another for support, not releasing his grip on the first until he was secure to the next.

Before long he was holding onto the platform's guardrail, just across from the unit; the marked access hatch was flanked by handholds. Reaching out, Donovich grabbed one, and then depressed the spring-loaded latch pin on the hatch, which opened with a snap. He swung it up until it locked. Inside was the unit's hardwired controls with its oscilloscope-style display showing two color-coded, opposing harmonic waveforms—normally it was just a straight line, indicating that all three axial oscillations were being effectively countered—but now one was out of sync.

"By the book," muttered Donovich as he looked up at the interior of the hatch for the procedural check list; it took him a moment to sort through the different emergency scenarios. "One: Check for manual setting change at panel." He looked down at the instrument panel, mostly back-lit in green; there were the three metal gear-tooth, wing-lock knobs in question. One was back-lit in red. "That's it!" he said.

To the side of the panel was the maintenance log—the Techs from the *Vandenberg* had recalibrated the system to compensate for the loss of two of the ship's external fuel tanks—the last entry was less than a day old.

"Right," he said as he reached for the knob. Its safety-lock worked like a prescription bottle's child-proof cap; with a determined squeeze to its side-wings, Donovich ever so gently turned the knob to the recorded setting. Like a concluding drumbeat, the pulsating stopped.

"...and all was right with the world!" he said with relief. Holding his hand still, he opened his fingers. The knob's locks pressed out and clicked; its backlight turned green.

He just stood there for a moment, looking over the instrument display, checking the lockdowns for any other possible problems.

"Chief, I take it you have things under control?" asked Ware over the comm.

"Yes, ma'am," rasped Donovich. His mouth and throat were a mess. "Right now, it looks like a switch shook loose; it's going to take us the better part of a day to look over the key systems to confirm that's the only problem."

"Very well, keep me informed; Ware out."

With a tap, he once again switched his comm to stand-by, then withdrew a marker from his pocket.

Dutifully, Donovich recorded the malfunction and setting change on the maintenance log; the computer entries would have to wait. His next stop was the medical supply cabinet, or med-station. Distracted by the thought of impending relief, he let his marker once again get away from him. It fell somewhere into the recessed area of the panel. "Butt-monkeys," he exclaimed.

Carefully he moved his head in for a look—the last thing he wanted was to bump something and start the show all over again. The marker wasn't in the front. Retrieving his pocket flashlight, he depressed the base switch; the LED cluster came to life.

Moving in close, he could only bring one eye to bear past the frame of the access hatch; he played the spot into the side portion of the recess. At first the stowaway didn't register—since he was preoccupied with looking for the marker. Once it did, he was feeling too crappy to really care either way. Things do manage to get onboard ship, but generally they don't last long in the inorganic environment of the module. "Great, and me without a mayonnaise jar," he said, with a feeling of annoyance at having something else to deal with.

His unwanted visitor was a spider, just sitting there at an odd angle, affixed to the instrument panel.

"Why is it always a spider, don't the cockroaches have a space program?" he said sarcastically.

As house spiders went, it was pretty big, maybe as much as an inch across, but it was hard to judge; his new friend was all bunched up, and Donovich's eyes were still a bit fuzzy.

Letting out a long breath, he thought over his options and decided upon the ancient, tried-and-true approach—the one that did not involve a newspaper.

He did, however, need something to store the beastie in. Donovich pulled the unused biohazard bag from his pocket, and with a practiced hand, swiped it full of air. Placing his flashlight into his mouth, he bit down on its flexible grip; he could feel the tension in his jaw rising along the left side of his aching face.

Rubbing his gloved fingertips together, Donovich explored whether he would have enough sensitivity not to squish the beastie—which would require him to dismantle the unit's casing to clean up the mess—let alone be able to catch it just by feel. The suit's gloves were state-of-the-art for working in vacuum; highly flexible, heated, and armored against puncture, so taking one off to reach blindly into a confined space, to grab a potentially poisonous spider, was out of the question.

Slowly he reached in, palm down and fingers fanned out; aiming for the mental image of the beastie's position. "I bet when I turn you over, you'll have 'Property of the *Vandenberg*' stenciled on your butt," he said.

Now beyond the controls, he slid his hand along the surface of the panel. Then he touched something with the side of his index finger, with a pinch, he tried to catch it against his thumb.

It felt slick—not wet—more like the effect you get when you bring equal poles of a magnet together, a sort of wavy feeling. Then it popped free and was gone. With his head starting to pound against the pressure in his jaw, Donovich withdrew his hand and took the light from his mouth.

Looking back in, Donovich saw that the beastie was still sitting in the same spot. "Now you're just messing with me," he said. This time around he noticed that the spider had thick, antenna-like protrusions coming from where its head should be, kind of like a cylinder with round ends. *Sort of hotdog-shaped*, he thought.

What he originally thought of as fur turned out to be either a glossy, blue-grey skin or a carapace, which meant it wasn't a spider, but whatever it was, it was hefty for its size. *What are you?* The very thought added to his headache; looking back over his shoulder, he could see the med-station in the distance, with its beautiful, six-pointed blue and white "Star of Life," which seemed to call to him. "I'll deal with you later," he said as he closed and snap-locked the unit's access hatch. Flattening the biohazard bag, he tucked it in a pocket and went to find some relief.

"I was enjoying myself earlier," he commented as he stood in front of the med-station's closet-sized door; he removed his comm-hood and let it hang by the suit's interface cable, he then ran a hand over his buzz-cut hair before opening the cabinet.

"Nothing is ever simple," grumbled Donovich as he looked at the maze of labeled, numbered, and color-coded drawers, compartments, and lock-boxes; unfortunately, he knew from experience where to find what he needed. He snapped a cold-pack to life and balanced it on his head while he dug out a tube of chewable pain killers.

As he was popping open the package's safety cap, he thought he heard something. Taking out several pills and slipping the rest into his pocket, he turned to face the gangway. He listened for anything beyond the usual sounds of the module; there was nothing. With the pills now dissolving in his mouth, it was time to get back to his station and finish off his coffee; he felt in his guts that this was going to be a very long day.

He had only taken a few steps when the sound of a dull thump echoed from somewhere in the module. *Must be Patterson moving about,* he thought, reaching for the comm control at his arm.

A distant crack and a sizzle caught his attention—the dreaded sound of something electrical arcing and shorting out. No alarm had sounded...yet. He quickly looked around his immediate area for any telltale signs of arc light or smoke.

The arcing sound had stopped, to be followed by a splat sound very nearby. With a hand holding the cold-pack in place, he was looking up through the deck gratings when something moved at the edge of his vision. Turning, he caught sight of it. Something steaming hot oozed down through the grating from the deck above.

Donovich moved toward it, being damn sure not to get underneath. Every fluid used onboard ship was color-coded and often scent-infused— like the sulfur they added to natural gas—this to alert the engineers to its threat level and possible system of origin; but this stuff was dark amber in color, and moved in a thick ribbon, like some form of industrial grease. It was already seeping through the deck grating at Donovich's feet. There was the smell of ozone in the air, and something almost sweet, like a marshmallow burnt black over an open fire.

Fear grabbed at Donovich as his imagination broke loose. The parallels to an old sci-fi movie raced through his mind; he suddenly felt vulnerable and naked against the unseen, but envisioned, horrors, moving about through the machinery of the module. Escape was out of the question; whatever was there was between him and the main hatchway to the CM.

As he backed away from the steaming goo, he struck his elbow on a protruding piece of equipment. The cold-pack dropped to the deck as he cradled his arm against the pain. Reality finally fell back in upon him.

"I need a nap," he said, moving his arm to work out the ache. He watched his hand, as he fanned and contracted the fingers against the numbness and tingling sensation. After retrieving the cold-pack from the deck, Donovich put on his comm-hood and secured the pack beneath it.

After a few more pain killers, he started off toward the ladder well, and the two-story climb to the life-boat deck. At this point he knew clearly that he should at least let Patterson know what was going on, but after his moment of insanity, he needed to make sure before he made a complete fool of himself. "Besides, if it eats my brain..." he laughed, "...then at least my headache will be gone." He started climbing.

From the ladder well he could see that whatever the goo was, it had dripped down from the top deck, through an intervening deck, to where he'd spotted it. He knew that there was no machinery in that general area of the life-boat deck, nor any hydraulic or fuel lines; only storage lockers.

The life-boat deck was designed to be used as an emergency staging area, in case the CM became compromised and had to be abandoned. To that end, it was basically just a large, open area ringed by stocked storage lockers.

On this trip it had been used as a barrack for two squads of Starine Ground Observers that had been dropped off over Demeter in re-entry capsules. As happens when people are thrown together out of necessity, Donovich came to know many of the men living on the life-boat deck. In fact, it was the GO team leader, Sergeant Ryan Warwick, who had warned the *Garryowen* of the impending missile strike. "Thanks, my friend," Donovich whispered.

"Get your mind back in the game," he ordered himself, as he neared the top of the ladder well. He could see where the unidentified fluid had come through the decking; sighting on that point, he casually brought his eyes above the level of the deck plating. There, caked onto the wall, was a line of goo running down from one of the chest-high lockers. Its door hung partially open.

With his feet still on the ladder's rungs, he took a slow and careful look around; this while visions of procuring something from the small arms locker continued to play across the back of his mind. "And I'm going to do what, to whom, with a Peacemaker?" he said, shaking his head in disbelief at his own foolishness, as he stepped onto the deck.

Despite the reticulating fans, the air was still thick with the sickly-sweet smell. As he walked slowly toward the locker, he wished that he had brought up his MAC suit's helmet, if for nothing else than an added feeling of security; then he remembered that it didn't help that guy in the movie. "Stop that," he forcibly whispered to himself.

Now, standing in front of the locker, he pulled it open by the handle and stepped back, keeping the door between him and whatever was inside. With a splat, something fell out onto the deck at his feet. Despite his best effort at self-control, Donovich jumped, his whole being riveted on what had landed in front of him.

There they sat, two baseball-size hemispheres, clearly parts of one whole, steaming and partially impaled by the corrugated decking. Like the goo, they were dark amber in color, except for where a lighter, fleshy material showed through from the areas torn open in the fall.

Donovich forced his breathing to slow, then held one breath and slowly let it out; he felt dizzy from the effort. His body awash with adrenalin and hormones, fueling him for either fight or flight against the unknown.

"Enough of this crap," he snapped, now becoming angry with himself. He swung the door open until it locked back, then stepped around the stuff on the deck to get a look inside the locker. After just a moment, Donovich stepped away and engaged the squad-ban. "Patterson from Donovich," he commed. A smile of relief crept across his face. He turned and walked toward the mess-station for something to drink.

"Yes, Chief?" replied Patterson.

"What's your location?"

"I'm 'n the machine room just below the middeck hatch."

"Come up to the life-boat deck," Donovich instructed, understanding that it was a six-story ladder climb. "I'm going to need help with a few things."

"Yes'ir," replied Patterson, almost enthusiastically; with a beep, the comm switched to standby.

Donovich felt physically rung out, and emotionally less than worthy to wear the uniform of the Aerospace Command. The only up-side to all this was that the mission recorders—the ship's black boxes—continuously stored system data and comm traffic, but only recorded images at very specific moments, such as Transition, and when certain alarms were tripped. So with luck, it should have missed all his stupidity over the stuff from the locker.

"Ya'll called, Chief?" said Patterson, as he climbed up onto the deck.

At about six-foot four and built like someone who worked for a living, Patterson literally stood out among his fellow Starmen.

Donovich just stood there by the open looker, sucking something from a collapsible drink bottle. "Is this your handy work, Sergeant?" he asked with an I-already-know-the-answer undertone.

Patterson just smiled and walked over for a better look. After a moment of contemplation, "Nice trick," he said turning to Donovich, "Someday ya'll have to tell me how I did it." Patterson had one of those easy-going personalities that made it hard not to immediately take a liking to him, but as far as Donovich was concerned, it was the fact that he was a highly knowledgeable and dedicated member of the engineering team that made him a worthwhile comrade.

Clamping the drink bottle closed, Donovich stowed it in his utility jumper and reached into the locker. "So you're claiming this isn't one of your practical jokes?"

"Yes'ir," Patterson replied. "My jokes never involve havin' to clean up afterward." He smiled and motioned toward the deck. "That's quite a smell you got there, what's this stuff?"

Donovich pulled out what appeared to be a closed pull-top can, and casually tossed it to Patterson; it was heavy and made a sloshing sound. Patterson turned it around in his hands for a look at the label. "Yellow Cling Peaches," he read.

"Yep, in heavy syrup; that explains the burnt-sugar smell," Donovich said as he pulled several other cans from the locker and placed them on the deck. "They're not Squadron-issued, so where did we get them?"

Patterson thought it over in his usual, drawn-out way; he once had to explain this to a rather annoyed instructor, "Sir, I'd rather be right and considered slow, than fast and stupid." Although this wasn't tolerated in training, it later proved to be one of his most outstanding attributes.

"I'd say it's part of the ship's discretionary cargo, most likely from one of the officers; hey, maybe even the CO?" he speculated.

"Lovely," stated Donovich, as he dug out several cleaning packs he had brought back from the kitchen station. "Well it's our mess now, let's get this done," he said, handing Patterson a pack.

Inside the locker was a mass of caramelized sugar and two more burnt peach halves. Donovich scooped the mess into a bag, and wiped down the area; the pack's chemically treated cloth made short work of the remaining goo, but it uncovered something else: a circular outline matching the base of the can was burnt into the floor of the lockers.

"Patterson, look at this," he called.

Without a word, Patterson stood up and watched as Donovich tried to clean off the ring. "It looks like the can just flashed over," said Patterson. He was no longer smiling.

"Agreed," stated Donovich as he bent down and picked up the other peach cans. "I don't know what's going on, but until we get a chance to sort things out I'm securing these in one of the ordnance bunkers we installed for the Starines." He headed out across the deck. Patterson joined him.

The bunker looked like a black garbage can bolted to the deck by four spring-loaded shock absorbers. "Get the lid for me," asked Donovich.

"Yes'ir," Patterson replied as he undid the oversized wing nuts.

"Thanks," Donovich said. He placed the cans down into the drum designed for storing small arms ammunition and explosive ordnance—such as grenades. The bunkers were more than capable of containing and redirecting the force of such an explosion; this while the quilted lining burst, releasing a cloud of heat-absorbing particles to dampen down any fire.

"Okay..." said Donovich as they secured the drum's lid, "...we'll finish the cleanup, then you can help me track down the bug in the DFC unit."

"Yes'ir, but my diagnostic set is still down by my station, it'll take me a bit..." he started to explain. Donovich motioned for him to stop talking.

"No, no, I mean, an actual bug." He held up his fingers to indicate the size. "About this big; I came across it after the incident," he said. "It was just sitting there on the panel..." Donovich fisted his hands and brought them up to either side of his head "...watching me with an eyeless, hotdog-shaped head."

Patterson just stopped and stared at him; a dull expression crossed his face as his eyes seemed to be looking back at some point in his memory.

"Patterson?" said Donovich calmly; it was obvious that his comrade was in trouble, "Robert...Bobby, look at me..." He resisted the urge to physically reach out to him. Patterson's breathing became deep and drawn out; something was frightening him.

"Starman Patterson!" yelled Donovich with his best military bearing, "Look at me!" Patterson snapped to attention and fixed his eyes on Donovich; the look of wide-eye terror quickly faded.

"Sir," said Patterson, as he pulled himself together.

"Would you care to explain yourself, mister!?" commanded Donovich, hoping that by maintaining the pressure, he could work out what was upsetting his fellow Starman.

"Can't," replied Patterson.

"Can't or won't!?" demanded Donovich.

Patterson took deep breath, "Can't." Clearly Patterson knew that this answer was going to piss him off, but before Donovich could retaliate, "Sir…" Patterson said, holding up his hands in an effort to deflect the outburst. "Chief, can we stop playin' spacemen for a bit, and just talk?" Patterson asked, sincerely, with a look of concern in his eyes.

Donovich picked up on this. "Sure," he said, and pulled out his package of pain killers. He took one, and then offered the rest to Patterson.

"No thanks," the man said with a wave of his hand. He turned and looked down over the deck's guardrail at the DFC unit. "It was about two years ago now, I was the Assistant Chief Engineer onboard the *Boston*. Well, we were homeward bound from Proxima; about a day under drive we started havin' electrical problems."

"Isn't that run about a week?" asked Donovich.

"About that," he agreed. "You know, electrical shorts and loose couplin's are business-as-usual after Transition; but then equipment lockdowns were bein' found opened, or even missin' all together."

To Donovich, it sounded like a disgruntled Starman engaged in a bit of revenge sabotage, most likely to make someone else look incompetent.

"Then the shit really hit the fan. One of the support stanchions for the LI's laser canal broke loose. I don't have to tell you, if the gravity detector went out, findin' home would have been more a matter of religion than science." he turned to see Donovich's reaction.

All Donovich could do was nod in agreement. The Laser Interferometer was the only navigational aid the ship had under drive; its primary function was to detect the approach of a gravitational anomaly, namely a star or some other super massive object. Without it, navigation would have to rely on pure mathematics and a ballistic trajectory to determine when to turn off the drive, and that could lead—*had* led—to timing mistakes measured in hundreds of millions of miles.

"Mind you, by the end of day six, everyone was involved 'n tryin' to figure this thin' out. The CO ordered all nonessential crew to their bunks, while the XO handled it. Of course, by then there were only a few of us runnin' around." Patterson looked annoyed. "I understand what they were tryin' to do, but it backfired; stuff started happenin' faster than we could fix it. At that point the XO threatened us with court martial."

Donovich knew the next part. "And in a time of war, that could have added up to being spaced."

"Damn Skippy it could," Patterson agreed. "As for your bug friend," he said, gesturing toward the DFC. "We were just 'n hour or so from droppin' out of drive, when I heard somethin' shortin' out. By the time I figured out where it was comin' from, this big-ass thin', kinda like a crab..." he put both of his hands together at the thumbs, with fingers spread wide to show the thing's size, "...just came floatin' along like it was 'n zero-g."

"What did you do?" asked Donovich, feeling somehow very stereotypical at having asked that.

Patterson seemed to take offense at the question. "I didn't do a damn thin'," he responded, and lunged his hands at Donovich's face to make his point about being startled. "I called out over the comm for help. I had to tell that story repeatedly before I could get anyone to believe me; or at least I thought they did. By then we had come out of drive; we spent the rest of the trip tearin' everythin' apart lookin' for it."

"Let me guess..." said Donovich.

"Don't bother," replied Patterson, cutting him off. "It was just like when pilots made the mistake of reportin' UFO's back in the days. Without proof a saucer banged up your plane, you were screwed."

"Didn't the mission recorders pick anything?" asked Donovich.

"Nope," said Patterson, "Just me screamin' over the comm about a God damn bug." Patterson started to smile, "But I got lucky. They were short-handed for this little invasion of theirs..." Without concluding the sentence, he pointed at the DFC, "Let's go have a look at your friend." and started off for the ladder well.

"You know, Patterson..." said Donovich as he followed him, "...if this turns out to be one big catten prank, the quartermaster is going to have to issue me a new pair of boots."

Patterson just looked at him for a moment, "Why so, Chief?"

Donovich smiled, "Because I'll have lost one up your ass!"

Now on the main deck, Donovich stepped around Patterson and walked off. "Where're you goin'?" asked Patterson.

Motioning at his station, Donovich explained, "I have coffee to attend to; besides, you'll need to figure out what to put the wee beastie in once you catch it."

Without a word, Patterson turned and headed toward the equipment lockers.

Then the lights went out, dropping the module into a world of inky black, outlined by yellow and green night-glow strips, with pockets of blue-white LED emergency lighting.

"What now?!" exclaimed Donovich as he rushed to his station; a red icon flashed on the console's power flow schematic. "Patterson!" he shouted. "Something just tripped the breaker on main bus B!" Thoughts of Patterson's little friend tearing apart his ship pushed at him.

 Near the ladder well, a work light came on, it was Patterson putting on his head-lamp; its beam playing out across the space. "I'm on it," he shouted.

Donovich checked the fault indicator log on the breaker; he anticipated a power spike as the reason—static-electric build up was a common problem under drive—but the read-back told another story. "Patterson, don't engage the breaker!" shouted Donovich urgently as he left the station. "Don't engage the breaker; it's set to failsafe during a power loss, there's a break in the line!" Not hearing a response from Patterson, Donovich raised his arm to access the comm control at his forearm.

An explosion of sparks erupted from the deck below, as fire claxons sounded and their accompanying yellow strobe lights pulsed. "Shit!" yelled Donovich, as he ran for the ladder well; pressing his feet against the outside of the ladder's rails, he slid down and landed with a jolt on the deck below. Grabbing for his flashlight, he hurried for the nearest fire extinguisher.

Patterson had just reached the ladder to follow Donovich down when he heard an arcing sound, coming from the life-boat deck; looking up he saw brilliant flashes of blue light dancing off the surrounding metal work. "Not this time," he growled, as he started up the ladder instead.

It only took one short blast from the extinguisher to deal with the problem; but now Donovich had to clean up the foam to inspect and repair the damage.

"Chief Donovich, status report," commanded the XO over the comm.

Donovich put down the extinguisher before answering. "Everything is now under control, sir," he said as he played his light over the damage. "We had a short circuit that set off the fire alarms." The conduit's access plate hung open; one of the cables had a clean piece missing.

"Very well, Chief, please keep me informed; Koenig out."

"Sabotage," whispered Donovich, as he slowly turned, expecting to find Patterson standing behind him; the Starman was nowhere to be seen. "I hope for your sake, that your little imaginary friends are real." Then it dawned on Donovich that they were screwed either way. Shaking his head, he walked to the deck's ancillary control station, and with a tap turned off the alarms.

Against the ringing in his ears he could hear Patterson shouting. It took Donovich a moment to spot him through the deck grating. Patterson was jumping around on the top deck; his point of interest seemed to be the ordnance bunker. Then there was an arc flash, followed by the sound of metal striking metal, as if something had just been thrown and bounced off onto the deck, accompanied by more shouting.

Silhouetted against the emergency lighting, something jumped—no flew—across the void of the gangway some three stories up. Looking like a pointy starfish, it flew with its six legs outstretched; reflected light contoured across its smooth surface. It brought its legs forward, and landed without a sound, disappearing into the deck's support structure and conduits.

"Did you see it!?" demanded a voice; it was Patterson leaning over the guardrail. "Chief!" he shouted forcibly.

"Yes..." Donovich squeaked. He cleared his throat, "...Yes, I saw it!" he shouted back, not quite believing what he had just said; but yes, he had seen something.

A few minutes later, Donovich joined Patterson above; the climb up to the life-boat deck had been one of apprehension and controlled fear.

"Look at this," said Patterson holding what was left of a spanner; half of its gapped end was missing. "I took a swin' at the thin' when it was cuttin' into the bunker." He pointed at the deck-mounted drum; four of its six spring-loaded, over-pressure bolts had been cut away.

Donovich turned and looked down over the guardrail at the mission clock, its four-inch high numbers read 482 hours and 01 minutes, "We have to get this thing contained; we're only two hours in, there's no way we can keep this up for three weeks," stated Donovich.

"And where you goin' to put it?" Patterson said, gesturing toward the damaged ordnance bunker.

Good catting question, thought Donovich, as he looked around for both inspiration and the beastie.

Patterson walked up to him. "So what would they do in one of those sci fi stories you keep readin'?" Patterson asked sincerely.

Oh, just great! Now we are relying on the delusions of some writer to save our asses, thought Donovich. "Well typically, at a dramatically quiet point in all the screaming and running about, they try to blow it out an airlock." he said.

"There's no way we're goin' to get that thin' up the length of the CM and into the axial airlock; we can't even risk lettin' it out of this module!" proclaimed Patterson.

"Yeah, you're right," agreed Donovich, "But...we could try to get it into one of the re-entry pods; with the CM's gangway hatches locked, it couldn't get any farther than the pod-bay."

"What's to keep it from burnin' through the Can's hatch?" Patterson asked.

"What's keeping it from cutting its way into the CM now; or back into the fuel module, or even the reactor?" said Donovich, waving his arm about to emphasize his point. "Besides, once we get the hatches closed, we depressurize the causeway and it's trapped on the wrong side of hard vacuum!" he added, smacking a fist into his other hand.

Patterson paused, "Okay, Chief, I'm with'ya; but first, lock off your comm." Donovich knew he looked a bit confused. "Remember," Patterson explained. "The mission recorder tracks all comm traffic. If this works out, then we'll have proof sittin' 'n the can; if not..."

"If not...were screwed, but at least we'll have some level of deniability at our court martial," said Donovich, thinking back to Patterson's UFO reference; back then a pilot's radio report proved nothing—except when they were used as evidence against his competency to continue flying—and these logs will prove nothing now; he smiled at Patterson and turned off his comm.

"So how do we do this?" asked Donovich.

"Well we know it's after the peach cans, so we'll put them 'n the pod, some place hard to get to 'n order to slow it down while I move up and close the hatches," said Patterson.

"No. For one thing you're too big to move around quickly in the pod-bay." Patterson started to object, but Donovich motioned for him to be quiet. "Secondly, I don't think it will be stupid enough to just crawl into the pod, after all, it set up a diversion to get at them the first time."

"Okay, Chief," Patterson agreed. "So then, we'll need somethin' to knock or blow it into the Can."

"Maybe rigging a quick valve to an O2 or nitrogen tank, with a piece of pipe big enough to hold one of the cans; when it climbs up, I pull the line on the valve..."

"Nope, too complicated," Patterson interrupted. "Get me one of those Growlers out of storage."

It took Donovich a moment to work it all out, but he saw where Patterson was going with this. "Right, I'll meet you back here."

"Do ya'll need a hand with that?" asked Patterson as Donovich came up the ladder one-handed, cradling a wastepaper bucket-sized canister in his arm.

"I'm fine," he replied and stepped out onto the deck.

Patterson was busy loading the peach cans into a utility bag; he already had an engineer's carryall tool-pack over his shoulder. "I was goin' to pop open one of these cans and..." The look on Donovich's face said volumes about the idea. "Okay, Chief," said Patterson, while making a calm-down gesture. "I didn't. I was just tryin' to figure out what it wanted with them."

Donovich had already played with the idea that it—or they—had come aboard in the cans, but somehow it didn't quite make sense; it was too easy an answer. So maybe it has something to do with the material makeup of the cans themselves; but what was it about an Alluna (Lunar Aluminum) can that made it so all-important? After all, most of the ship was built from the stuff in one grade or other.

Patterson stood up and slung the utility bag over his shoulder. "You ready?"

Donovich nodded. "Any sign of our friend?" he asked, looking about.

"Couldn't rightly say," replied Patterson, as he depressed the 'hatch open' button on the station's console. Pulsating yellow lights flared to life and the chirping alert tones seemed louder than ever. Both men looked around, anxiously awaiting the inevitable appearance of the beastie.

"Go," instructed Patterson.

The hatches weren't even locked back yet and Donovich was up, though, and standing at the pod-bay's hatch controls.

With one last look around, Patterson scurried up the ladder. "Push it!" he yelled, even before clearing the opening. Donovich held it for just a moment before engaging. The inner hatch closed with a thump, its indicators switching to a steady-red.

The pod-bay was a cramped toroid shape; its empty ordnance racks curved along the surface of the bay's wall. At some point in time, the powers-that-be decided this would be a good place to mount the ship's automated point-defense cannons. So, protruding from both the ceiling and floor there were the butt ends of the turrets, with brightly colored warning labels and yellow and black cross-hatching around each of the weapons' ammunition feeds. But since the *Garryowen* was now out of the fight and heading home—as per operational doctrine—her ammunition stores were off-loaded and would be used as a reserve for the remaining ships in the squadron. *We're not paid to bring it home with us,* thought Donovich.

"I don't know how much time it's going to give us," said Donovich, "So I'll prep the pod. Here's your quarter-of-a-million-dollar toy." He handed the cylinder to Patterson in exchange for the utility bag. "Remember, it comes out of your pay."

Patterson just smiled and nodded. Carefully, he placed the cylinder on the deck before taking off and opening the tool pack. "Chief, lock the CM hatch; we don't want Koenig buzzin' around," said Patterson.

"No problem."

Patterson flipped over the black cylinder. Its yellow stencil markings indicated that it was a "MK 42 SLD," along with a series of inventory tracking and ID numbers. With a practiced hand, he removed the electronic decoy's baseplate and unfastened its separator charge; he looked it over, and then said a quick prayer before continuing.

With a click, Donovich inserted the failsafe pin into the pod's docking port control panel—this physically locked the port's docking clamps, while electronically overriding the pod's launch program—the T-handled pin had the traditional foot-long "Removed Before Flight" ribbon dangling from it.

According to the manual, "...if a pod were to be launched while a ship was under drive; upon impact with the drive field, the pod would atomize, the resulting energy flux would cause the drive field to collapse and drop the ship out of hyperspace, not unlike a conventional Return Transition."

Donovich's only problem with this answer was simple, "To date no one has tried it," and he wasn't about to be the one in the history books to find out.

"Damn right," he said. Reaching back, he grabbed the utility bag and pushed it into the causeway.

"You set?" ask Donovich, as he crawled out a few minutes later.

"Just about, if you'd give me a hand," Patterson responded, as he held the charge up against the framework for the gun's autoloaders.

"Right." Donovich held the charge in place while Patterson zip-tied it down.

"What's going to happen when this thing goes off?"

Patterson screw-connected a spool of wire to the charge. "It'll just pop, and hopefully launch the peach can into the Can with our friend sittin' on it," he said. "It's a gas separator charge, works just like a car airbag. You can let go."

"Thanks."

Donovich moved off to ready the other pod; Patterson followed behind, playing out the wires.

With the starboard pod now locked down and hatches opened, Patterson ran his wires up into it; then, with the AeroCom equivalent of a roll of duct tape, he secured and camouflaged the wires to the deck. "Right, get 'n," he said.

Donovich got down on his hands and knees and backed into the darkened pod; he lay on his stomach, propped up on his elbows, just behind the hatch in the causeway; Patterson squatted down and handed him a circuit tester to which he had connected the wires from the charge.

"You know how this works," stated Patterson. "Key the power on, then hold," he said, indicating the recessed red test button.

Donovich just nodded. "See you afterward."

"Yep," replied Patterson; he then stood up and walked over to the charge, placing a can of peaches into the clamps that normally held the decoy secure. He watched as Donovich pulled his pod's access hatch closed on the wires.

The sight of Patterson disappearing down the ladder into the SM filled Donovich with a sense of abandonment; as an engineer, being physically alone for long periods on shift was business as usual, but he always knew there was someone else on the other end of the comm to come to his aid.

This time, it was just him and the universe; waiting in the dark, while looking through a small porthole window into the lit pod-bay, half hoping that the damn creature didn't show up.

Time passed. How long, it was hard to say; Donovich just kept looking through the porthole at the open gap of the SM's two-meter hatchway. From time to time, phantoms would startle him, as his mind turned passing shadows and random sounds from the service module into the approach of the unknown.

There comes a point when fatigue wins out over fear, and the need to rest becomes all important; Donovich was already there. The urge to yawn kept forcing him to lower or angle his head away from the porthole for fear of fogging it up.

"Damnit," he whispered, as he wiped his eyes; looking back into the pod-bay his mind said, *something is out there*. His breathing shallowed as his fear grew more tangible. There it was, slowly crawling around the edge of the hatchway. They had thought that it would try another diversion; but no, stealth was its new game plan.

Once in the bay, it stopped. It just stood there, clinging against the curvature of the wall; slowly, it started moving with spider-like locomotion toward the port pod. It looked just like the little one he had found in the DFC unit, but if it was, it had grown to almost a foot across. It stopped at the edge of the pod's causeway, its hotdog-like head flexed, as if it was looking around; it seemed to be contemplating their trap. With surprising speed, it darted into the pod.

Just like an ungrateful monster...thought Donovich as he slowly opened his hatch; he was trying desperately to be quiet as he crawled out on his elbows and knees, the circuit tester still in his hand. Now clear and standing, he could see past the loader's framework into the pod. There was no sign of the creature; hopefully it was still under the seats trying to dig out the cans.

He needed to keep his eyes on the pod, but he also had to be careful where he walked; now under gravity he could easily fall through the SM's open hatchway. He briefly looked down to check his position. It was strangely quiet in the SM. Patterson wasn't in sight.

Donovich was just coming around the loader when the creature came back into view; he froze at the thought of rushing the pod, and then he remembered that he hadn't keyed on the circuit tester. Without looking he brought his other hand to the box and turned the key.

The beastie spun and leapt down the short length of the causeway at him. There was a boom as the gas charge went off, knocking Donovich aside. As he sat there, he realized that his thumb was firmly pressing down on the test button.

Dropping the box, he scrambled to the hatch. The beastie wasn't in the causeway. With everything he had left, he lifted the hatch into place. It stopped just short of closing. The beastie's six pointy, blue-gray legs popped from around the edge of the hatch.

"Shit!"

He suddenly found the adrenalin-powered strength to push. His shoulder drove into the hatch. Without forethought of the consequences, he smashed his fist down at the nearest leg. The hatch snapped shut and locked as his hand connected. The beastie had pulled back.

Breathing hard, Donovich just knelt there, both hands needlessly pushing on the hatch. Carefully, he looked through the porthole; the beastie just sat there, all bunched up, as he had seen before. Its hotdog head slowly flexed.

"Donovich!" Patterson shouted, as he frantically climbed into the pod-bay; he stopped when Donovich turned and looked at him. Carefully, Patterson knelt down next to him; he reassuringly put a hand on Donovich's shoulder, before looking through the porthole.

"I didn't get the pod's hatch closed, just the bay's." said Donovich, concern and exhaustion coloring his voice, as he gestured over his shoulder.

Patterson turned to him, "It's okay, Chief." he said calmly, "I'll deal with it. It's almost over, but you need to go tell Ware what's happenin'." He half-pulled Donovich to his feet. The Chief resisted. All he wanted to do was close his eyes and pretend none of this had happened.

"It's got to be you, Chief, you're the guy in charge," Patterson insisted, as he unlocked the CM's gangway hatch; it opened with the usual lights and sound. Sluggishly, Donovich nodded and started up the ladder.

Patterson returned to the pod. The beastie—as the Chief called it—was stretched out over the porthole. "Dear God!" he said. The creature's legs, and in fact all of its different body parts, weren't physically connected. They just seemed to stay in place like some stylized, computer-generated cartoon character.

Patterson leaned back and eyed the docking port's emergency pod jettison controls. Calmly, he reached up and removed the failsafe pin. The panel lit up as a warning klaxon sounded that the pod's inner hatch was still open. He lifted the cover over the manual override switch and threw it. With his hand on the jettison pull bar, he looked back through the porthole.

The creature had pulled back; its eyeless, cylinder-like head was staring back at him. Patterson leaned into the porthole "You're not fuckin' me over again," he said as a little smile grew across his face, "You don't exist," he whispered....

The late great storyteller CJ Henderson dared Dani to write this story during a long car ride on their way to a convention. The conversation centered on comfort zones in writing and how to break out of them. CJ's challenges were never to be taken lightly. The result, a Lovecraftian romance in space, made the old man proud. May you enjoy the story as much as she squirmed to write it...

Greg Schauer

IN THE DYING LIGHT

Danielle Ackley-McPhail

Earth Orbit: 42.05.18 – 0715hrs

On the command deck of the Stellar Clipper *McKay*, First Officer Ushimi Yakata ran the final checklist before third shift ended:

Duty Log: 42.05.18 – 0715hrs, Yakata, U.
Reactor status – nominal;
O_2 levels – optimal;
Power – five percent over-consumption.

She frowned at the last item as she printed out a hard copy of the entry. *We're going to have to watch our calculations,* she thought. *We haven't even left orbit and already the systems are running hot.*

It was that damn shuttle Corporate had them balancing on the *McKay*'s nose. They were hauling the spacer's equivalent of a luxury yacht over twelve light years to Demeter just so some CEO could tour his colonial facilities in style...There were much more important payloads they could have taken with them. Of course, it was the "pay" part that decided things in the end; the rates for transporting luxury items to the Tau Ceti system were ten times that of necessary goods.

Behind her a *clunk* and a soft *whoosh* announced the arrival of her replacement. A whiff of licorice drifted from close by her ear. She'd stopped counting the times she had told Karl Dunn not to crowd her. A prime example of why they had a history and no future. She'd had doubts about signing him for this cruise. They had been close once, very close. But not anymore. And with only a nine-man crew, she had no hope of avoiding him.

Her lips pressed in a tight, thin line, Yakata dropped her hand to the toggle by her hip and shifted the command chair back along its track, away from the control panel.

"Hey! Watch it!"

She brought the chair around, her grey eyes leveled dead on at Karl as he rubbed his abdomen where the chair smacked into him. Only his grip on the nearby tether bar kept him bobbing in place.

"Excuse me," she said, her tone cool and formal. "I didn't realize you were so close."

The flat, persistent tone of the proximity warning sounded through the cabin, interrupting any comment Karl would have made. They both forgot their personal conflict, their attention riveted on the sensors.

Toggling the command chair back into place, Yakata automatically scanned the ship's attitude and power consumption on the screens flanking the main monitor. At the same time, she called up the isometric collision display. The flashing alert icon vanished from the screen in front of her. In its place appeared a wire-frame sphere with a representation of the *McKay* in the center. Something closed on the ship from behind, moving at a fraction of a meter per second. They had about thirty minutes until it came into range over their drive section.

"Dunn, reach over and activate the aft camera," Yakata ordered as her fingers danced in and out of the button depressions on the control panel. At her command, the main display switched from short-range to long-range scanning. She had to be sure whatever approached was not the forward edge of a meteor storm or something else their ablative hull plating could not handle.

Her scans told her nothing more. She called to Karl, "Crewman, do we have visual?"

Silence.

"Crewman..." Her short, sharp tone telegraphed impatience. "Do...we... have...visual?"

She whipped around, spearing him with a glare. He remained oblivious, his feet tucked into the boot docks and his gaze riveted on the image on the external monitoring station.

What the hell? Yakata had never seen him like this. He looked stunned...horrified. What could be out there?

Remembering the fate of her father's freighter, the *Tyler*, she felt a shiver of dread. Not another wreck...

She couldn't tell; Karl's body blocked the screen. Impatiently, she released the restraint keeping her in the command chair and drifted out. Once she cleared the panel, she rotated and pulled herself toward Karl.

"Step aside, crewman," she barked.

His intent gaze snapped to her. Emotions rippled violently across his face, darkening his deep brown eyes to nearly black. It unsettled her, but Yakata didn't back off. Dunn's moods were nothing new to her. He had always been too on edge, his emotions close to the surface; like he picked up on random vibes in the air that no one else could feel. In their time together, she had never been able to tell what a given situation would trigger. Now she told herself she didn't really care. She kept her expression impassive and her gaze sharp. "Move it...now."

The muscles along Karl's jaw twitched and his eyes fell out of focus. He closed them and gave his head a little shake. She could see the tension drain away. When he opened his eyes again, they reflected faint confusion. Without a word, he gave the standard heel jerk to free his feet from the workstation's dock and drifted off to the side.

She gave him a measured look before redirecting her attention to the screen. The camera completed deployment, the high-power, one-hundred-optical zoom fully engaged. What a stunning view. Distant stars glittered like metallic flecks on a field of raw black silk and muted colors added an unexpected depth to the starscape. Pretty sights didn't interest her, though. She scanned for her objective with an intensity that mirrored Karl's earlier stance.

The projectile headed toward them wasn't some random bit of space debris; it was clearly manufactured. The shape appeared something like a squat pillar or obelisk, and appeared to be about the size of her head. It was too far away to make out much more, though the camera hinted at intricate detail.

Rogue thoughts of her father swarmed her mind once more. In his last letter to her, he mentioned a similar find. She'd lost him long before the letter ever reached her. Neither her father, nor the object had been retrieved. Burned into her memory, as clear as yesterday, was the image of his shattered helmet found floating in the vacuum of space. She still had that helmet.

She banished the thought. Turning back to Karl, Yakata caught his eye and held it. "Assume your post. I'm heading up to the rendezvous station to retrieve the object."

He remained silent a moment. His jaw ticked and his gaze flickered from the aft display to her face.

"'Ta…" he began, but she cut him off.

"Excuse me, crewman, how did you address me?"

"Ma'am," he ground out through clenched teeth, frustration snapping in his eyes. "Respectfully, I'm not sure that you should… something feels really wrong about this."

"I have to do this."

The knowing look he gave her disconcerted Yakata. If anyone understood, he did. She didn't like that familiarity or the self-betraying warmth she felt at his concern. "I said get to your post. Start the pre-hyperdrive checklist," she ordered. "The captain wants to jump by 0800."

She pulled her communications hood up over her close-cropped ebony hair and triggered the overhead hatch. With the grace of frequent practice, she hauled herself up through the shaft. Propelling herself past the T-junction that branched off toward the cargo bay, she opened the second hatch into the rendezvous station. She closed it behind her before drifting toward the aft window. Yakata pressed the activation button on the left side of her comm hood. "Command deck…"

A sharp chirp sounded before Karl responded, his voice slightly staticky. "Go ahead, ma'am."

"I need an update on the incoming object."

There was a pause. While she waited, Yakata peered out into space, as if she had any chance of pinpointing the object without the aid of the cameras. It drew closer, but not that close.

Another chirp brought her out of her distraction.

"Ma'am?"

"Go ahead, crewman."

"The object is ten minutes out and closing."

"Acknowledged," she responded, and cut the connection.

Ten minutes. Barely enough time to deploy the arm. She snapped her boots into the docks and engaged the control panel. Powering up the arm, she then hit the sequence instructing it to retrieve the grappling attachment. While the mechanism prepared, she triggered the cargo bay doors. A strident warning klaxon sounded as a large segment of the ship opened to space. The arm rose from its cradle in slow, precise movements. Her teeth gritted and her muscles tensed as she watched. It had to move faster or she would miss the interception point. With her free hand, she depressed the activator on her comm hood once more.

"Command deck..."

"Go ahead, ma'am."

"Feed me the trajectory of the object."

On the panel in front of her, a micro-display came to life. The information played across it. This was going to be close. She deployed the grappling net to intersect the flight path and held her breath. The object crested the drive section in a gentle arc, and seemed to flare as it came into contact with the sun's rays, bathing the ship and arm in a startling green glow. It faded in the shadow of the arm. Yakata leaned into the console. It appeared her prize might overshoot the net. Reaching for the joystick in front of her, she extended the assembly as high as it would go over the drive section.

Her breath hitched. It still looked at risk of skimming past. *This is ridiculous. It's space debris. There's no reason I should be so upset.* She tried shifting the joystick even further, but the arm had reached full extension.

Her father's face drifted unbidden across her thoughts. It felt like she had failed him...again. She clenched her teeth and forced the thought away. Furious blinking cleared her vision, but she could hardly believe what she saw: the object changed trajectory. The alteration was slight; barely perceptible except for the drive section acting as a point of reference. Still, Yakata had to wonder if she had really seen it. This was impossible. The thing could not have changed its trajectory. Short of mechanical means or an outside intervention, an object moving in space would continue along the same path until it encountered another force. And yet, as the artifact plowed into the grappling net, she forgot all about the laws of physics. The net closed, locking the object into place.

"Yeah!" she cried out, the sound loud and unbridled in the seclusion of the rendezvous station. Only the boot docks kept her from bouncing around the compartment. "Oh, yeah!"

A burst of unexpected static crackled from her comm hood. She felt the blood drain from her face as she went still.

"Hey! Knock it off!" Karl's amused voice came over the connection she'd forgotten to close. "You want to rupture my ear drum?"

"My apologies, crewman," she responded with a degree of dignity she did not currently feel. "The object has been retrieved. I'm locking down and securing the salvage."

She cut the connection.

Shoving embarrassment aside, Yakata input the sequence that returned the arm to its cradle. Another rapid set of keystrokes, and the cargo bay doors closed. She grew impatient with the drawn-out procedure. Recklessness in vacuum, however, could get a spacer killed.

Once everything was locked down, she retreated to the ante-chamber to climb into her protective constrictor suit. She waited for the green light from the automatic systems check before securing her helmet and engaging the O_2 tanks. Prepped for EVA, Yakata cycled through the airlock into the cargo bay.

She grabbed an empty storage container and hauled both it and herself down the length of the armature. Once there, she anchored the container to the deck and pulled herself up the handholds along the wall until she drew even with the grappling attachment. She hit the release and worked the fingers open.

Her hands twitched over the surface of the artifact and she had to resist the urge to draw off her suit's skin-tight gloves. The object demanded to be caressed.

In shape, it resembled a short, squat obelisk. It tapered slightly from top to bottom and had three columns of unfamiliar symbols running up and down each side. It was metal...apparently old metal, given the deep, dull sheen. The color had a greenish tinge, like ancient bronze. Only this was no metal she recognized. It seemed smooth, almost soft, other than the etching. Otherwise, there were no seams or depressions.

It took extreme effort to lower the thing into the bin. Now was not the time to examine it. She had less than ten minutes to get herself secured for hyperdrive. Unhitching the container, she hefted it to her shoulder and propelled herself toward the airlock. In the antechamber, she slid her burden into a storage locker by the cargo bay hatch and keyed it to her personal code. It would be safe until she could take it down to the lab.

Duty Log: 42.05.18 – 1100hrs, Kinney, Captain J.
Reactor status – nominal;
O_2 levels – 98 percent;
Power – ten percent over-consumption
Note: Schedule diagnostics of ship's systems upon arrival at Demeter, *McKay* exhibiting systems-wide reduction in efficiency despite recent overhaul. Power fluctuations ship-wide, stabilized. Malfunction of atmospheric filters in compartments 8A through C, corrected. Electrical fires between bulkheads 10 and 11, section 5, contained; damage minimal.

Cargo Bay Antechamber: 42.05.18 – 1100hrs

Yakata struggled for hours to get some rest. She just couldn't do it, though. The artifact haunted her thoughts. She would almost say it called to her, but that was as nuts as thinking it had changed its trajectory. She tossed and fussed until Jackson and Pittman, the crewmembers trying to sleep in the billets flanking hers, begged her to give up.

That was why she climbed back down into the cargo bay ante-chamber again. Captain Kinney, in position on the command deck, had given her a considering look, but didn't question her. She'd already briefed him about the events that occurred at the end of her shift.

All thought of anything but the artifact fled her mind as she pushed open the last hatch and continued down the ladder, which in orbit had been the floor. She hated the way hyperdrive and the artificial gravity it created turned reality perpendicular to orbital conditions. Kneeling down, she punched her code with rapid jabs and hauled open the storage locker at her feet.

Any thought of spatial geometry evaporated.

Yakata half expected the artifact to be a dream. But there it was, nestled in its bin. She tried to draw it out of the locker.

It wouldn't budge. In the weightlessness of the orbiting ship, the artifact had been nothing to move. Now that they were under drive there was artificial gravity again. Not earth-norm, but enough that they could walk on the deck. If the obelisk was this heavy in three-quarters grav, she didn't want to consider what it would be like under normal conditions. It had to be denser than gold.

No! Yakata straddled the opening, flexed her knees, and inch by inch pulled the container up, until sweat ran into her eyes and her muscles screamed. She was not waiting forty-eight hours until they were in orbit.

Personal Log Entry: 42.05.18 – 1230hrs, Dunn, K.

We retrieved something today. 'Ta...excuse me...First Officer Ushimi hasn't told me what it is. Don't think she even knows. While I was on shift, she took it to the storage bay Captain had temporarily converted into a lab. She talked O'Neal, the metallurgist we're shepherding to Demeter, into helping her try to figure out what it is.

She goes on shift in seven hours, but they're still holed up in that lab. She's going to be a real bitch on deck tonight if she doesn't get some sleep, but she's obsessing on that bit of debris.

Of course, I can't stop thinking about it either. It's gotten under my skin. It shouldn't be on this ship! It has me so freaked, and I can't even tell why. The first half-hour of my shift is a lost memory. All I know is that it feels like we are in for a major shitstorm.

Temporary Science Lab: 42.05.18 – 1230hrs

"What in the world made Corporate think it was worth the 100-million-dollar ticket to haul you up here?" Yakata growled through clenched teeth. Even as she said it, her hindbrain winced.

Bastian O'Neal, world-renowned metallurgist, lowered his instruments to the work surface and gave her a long, silent look. The dignified expression on his ebony face didn't change, but his hazel eyes were disapproving. He didn't answer. He looked away and took up the artifact in both latex-covered hands, repositioning it for another documenting photograph.

She'd strained to haul her prize down here; he seemed to toss it about as if it were cotton candy. Part of that was due to his clearly prosthetic left arm; but part had to be because of his own innate strength. Someone who didn't know better could be excused for thinking he mined metals, rather than studying them.

The metallurgist set aside his digital camera and picked up the item once more. He turned it in his hands until he'd looked at every side, his finger lingered over the engraving. She wanted to snatch it from his grasp. Uncontrollably, a muscle in her forehead twitched, as did her fingers. How dare he manhandle her salvage like that, hefting it with an ease that she couldn't? She tensed and fought not to scowl at him. What was wrong with her?

Yakata tried to shake it off. This was O'Neal's field. She'd come to him for help and he was kind enough to give it. She should be grateful and respectful, at the very least. It wasn't like her to behave this way. She took a deep breath and forced herself to calm, to offer an apologetic smile and be pleasant.

Finally, O'Neal set the artifact down. Yakata expected to relax. Instead, she tensed even more; ready, in fact, to hurry forward and grab the obelisk away. But then O'Neal spoke, distracting her.

"I can't identify it."

"What do you mean you can't identify it?!"

"The tests were unable to determine the age or composition of the material."

Her resolve to be polite evaporated. "What did Corporate do... send you up here as a tax write-off?"

Seething with frustration, Yakata grabbed for her artifact.

O'Neal stepped in her way.

"If you're done insulting me?

"There's one more test I can run, but I need some equipment from the storage bay. My imaging spectrometer is our last option on-ship."

She glared at him and had to force her negativity down. It was harder to do. Without a word, Yakata moved to the terminal set into the chamber wall, her feet straddling the boot docks.

The muscles in her shoulders bunched and tightened as she keyed in the commands calling up the ship's manifest. He watched her. Surely plotting to take her salvage for himself.

Whoa! Where did that paranoia come from? She forced it away.

Finally, she located his equipment and requested immediate retrieval. Closing out the screen, she whirled to face him. For a moment, everything held a greenish tinge like the one she'd noted when the object crested the drive section. The sense of looming increased with the glow. It faded so quickly, though, that she had to wonder if it were her vision causing the effect. That would explain the flickers out of the corner of her eye. Yakata clenched her eyes shut and popped her neck. It sounded like several rounds of gunfire.

"Sorry, O'Neal, can't imagine why I'm so edgy. Jackson will bring your spectrometer down in short order. Why don't you head to the mess for some coffee...I'll comm you when the equipment gets here."

"That's okay. If I'm here when it arrives I can hook it into the ship's systems quicker. This has already taken longer..."

"O'Neal," Yakata cut him off, her tone sharp and brittle, even to her own ears. "Go get some coffee. I'll have the spectrometer rigged up when you get here."

For a moment, she thought he would refuse. Her suspicions flared brighter and she had to consciously force her fists not to clench. She didn't trust him here; didn't want him here, unless he was in the middle of a test. Even then she had issues.

Her gaze again locked with his. She read concern in his eyes. But did something else lurk beneath that? Something sly? Calculating? Damnit! She couldn't tell! It took more effort to mimic something of a reasonable tone. "I have to be here to sign off on the retrieval. If you don't want any coffee, could you at least get me some? I'm dying here."

Temporary Science Lab: 42.05.18 – 1245hrs

Yakata vibrated with impatience as O'Neal finished calibrating the spectrometer. She wanted to snatch his hands away from the knobs and buttons and yell at him to get on with it. It wasn't just an overwhelming need to know. That she could have handled. No, it was more like whatever lurked behind her drew closer, just out of sight, just out of hearing range. Always there, always watching… Some part of her equated it with the artifact. She had to know what it was now, but the technology would do them no good if it weren't set up properly. She understood that.

Then why was she ready to scream when he slipped a common bit of steel in the spherical sample chamber and fired up the machine?

She couldn't restrain herself any more. "Come on, already!"

"Do you want accurate results, or do you just want me to go through the motions?" O'Neal's voice came out a low, controlled rumble, contrasting sharply with her outburst. "If you don't care if the results are accurate, you're wasting my time and I'm out of here."

His response made Yakata want to scream even more, but he was right. What was wrong with her? Her impatience did not serve either one of them well and she couldn't afford to have him abandon the test. She could probably figure out the machine, but the data it spit out would be indecipherable to her.

Taking a deep breath, she forced herself to calm.

"Sorry."

It took a lot of effort not to fidget as O'Neal watched her closely a moment. The concern had returned, along with a thread of irritation. He clearly wanted this to be done as much as she did, even if their reasons were different. Without a word, he turned back to the spectrometer.

"Okay, we're ready."

Yakata's pulse sped up. She reached for the artifact, only to flinch back as a mild static arced between it and her fingertips. It seemed to cling to her hand like the persistent suction of vacuum through a hull breach. Like something tried to suck her out the tiniest hole, only the hard surface of reality kept her from going through. Before she could say something, the pull abruptly released and a surge of rage and frustration swelled over her. She shook it off. Looked up in a daze. O'Neal had lifted her prize away and slid it into the chamber in place of the metal bar. He made no comment and Yakata saw no sparks when he touched it. Had the phenomenon been her imagination? She couldn't resist creeping forward to glance at the operator's display as the spectrometer charged up to pulse full-spectrum light at the object from six points within the sphere.

The hum of the machine seemed to come up through the deck plates until she expected her entire body to vibrate with it. A flaring light intensified abruptly until it engulfed the machine and the room. The power surged and the deck plates vibrated more violently beneath Yakata's feet. Both she and O'Neal flinched in that instance of brilliance before they were engulfed by utter darkness. The only sound was a sharp gasp. She couldn't tell which of them it came from. She could no longer hear the spectrometer or any of the ship's normal background mechanical noises. Other than their nervous breathing, silence dominated the pitch black.

Yakata struggled not to panic. Where was the hum of the hyperdrive? The click of relays opening and closing? The sizzling snap of the comms? Sounds every spacer took for granted; their unrealized security blanket in everlasting night.

Yakata shuddered.

The darkness seemed to last forever; in truth it was less than twenty seconds before systems re-engaged with a whir. Not even long enough for them to fall out of drive.

Right on the heels of everything powering up, all comms within hearing distance gave a strident chirp.

"...eport...All crew, report!"

She reached for the comm on the console and toggled the activator to respond to Captain Kinney.

"Yakata here. O'Neal and I are in the Science Lab."

"What the hell was that?"

Yakata didn't have an answer. She couldn't have gotten one in, anyway, as a stream of responses came over the comm. All crew were accounted for.

"Everyone to stations, run full diagnostics. Let's figure out what the deal is before it happens again," Captain Kinney ordered before closing the comm line.

Turning to O'Neal, Yakata noted the confusion on his face as he looked at the read-out from the spectrometer.

"What? Something go wrong?"

O'Neal turned toward her, his head shaking. "The test completed before everything shut down, but this doesn't make sense."

She walked over and read the printout:

Processing Error 021:
Spectral Anomaly – Negative Scan

"Kuso shite shinezo!" Yakata hissed through clenched teeth.

O'Neal looked at her oddly. "I don't know what you just said, but it sounded painful."

Yakata flushed. Among spacers cursing was one thing, profanity was a part of their make-up. But in front of others she generally conducted herself more circumspectly. She was just grateful the man did not speak Japanese.

"I apologize for my rudeness. But, damn!" She slammed her hand down on the casing of the machine. "All of that and it's unidentifiable!"

"Not just unidentifiable...it's like nothing's there. The machine didn't even register the walls of the chamber." His expression grew considering. "It's as if the artifact absorbed the light. But to do so this completely...it's impossible for none to have gotten past it."

"Malfunction?"

"Not one I've ever seen, but there's one way to find out."

Captain Kinney had ordered everyone to their stations. But she had to know. She could always double-time it to the command deck.

O'Neal opened the chamber and reached for the artifact. He hissed sharply, as if in pain. His body arched and shuddered. The look of terror in his eyes sent panic through Yakata. It must be the prosthetic. She remembered the static that had clung to her hand when she'd touched the artifact earlier.

Yakata yanked an equipment bag toward her and rapidly rifled through it. Tucked in the bottom she found a set of insulated gauntlets. She donned them and braced herself against the workstation. With all her weight behind the effort, she hauled on the obelisk until it left his grasp. It came away with the sound of metal scraping metal. Yakata landed in a heap across the compartment, the obelisk heavy on her chest. O'Neal collapsed across the table, greenish static arcing and popping along the length of his arm. He shook his head and groaned. After a moment, he leveled a glare toward Yakata.

Perhaps it was the sparks, or perhaps just the light, but as he stared at her in silence, it seemed his eyes reflected the green hue. He slowly stood and stalked across the room to where she lay. When he reached out his hand, her eyes went wide, expecting pain.

She searched his face for some clue as the man remained silent. His eyes darkened and she couldn't read the swirl of emotions dancing through them. She shivered. He closed his eyes with a sigh. When he opened them all she saw was impatience in their green depth. Green? But....

"The gauntlets..."

She yanked them off and held them up, never taking her eyes from him. He donned the gear and lifted the artifact from her chest. She gasped as breath flooded back into her lungs to full capacity. Damn, that thing was heavy, she swore to herself.

O'Neal turned his back to her. He deposited the obelisk on a metal tray on the table and reinserted the control element he'd used to test the machine initially.

The second reading of the steel bar was identical to the first.

Without a word, Yakata returned the artifact to its storage locker. Using her body as a shield, she keyed the lock with her personal code.

She turned and found O'Neal staring at her. Yakata carefully slipped past him and hurried from the compartment, trying to ignore the faint odor of scorched latex lingering in her nostrils.

Personal Log Entry: 42.05.18 – 1250hrs, Dunn, K.

McKay's systems just flatlined. Everything's back up, but talk about freaking out. What the hell is going on?

Haven't felt like this since I was four and Da took me to the reptile house at the Bronx Zoo. I zoomed all over that place. Couldn't stay still...until I came to the king cobra. Something had pissed it off. It mantled and swayed three feet high in the air, right up close to the glass. It kept up a hiss, low and menacing. Don't know how long I stood there watching its tongue flicker in and out above me, but I couldn't move. Not even when it struck. Lightning-fast it slammed into the glass. To this day, I swear its fangs left long grooves in the surface, dripping with venom.

I still remember the stench of terror. Right now it's strong in my nose...a hundred times stronger than it was when I was four. And I have that feeling again...like death is hovering above my head and I'm not sure if the glass is going to hold.

Damn...Captain just called duty stations.

Command Deck: 42.05.18 – 1310hrs

Yakata hauled herself through the command deck hatch from the *McKay*'s main shaft into a tangible silence. The shaft ran the length of the ship and was fitted out with a ladder that doubled as a track for the slow-moving utility lift. The track could either be climbed or used for crewmen to pull themselves along, depending on the ship's attitude. She had scaled it at record speed, but apparently she hadn't been quick enough.

"First Officer Ushimi...the comm system may have been affected by the anomaly. My order to report to duty stations doesn't seem to have reached all compartments." The captain's words were even and void of tension. His gaze was not. The look he gave her was harder than the artifact she'd left in the lab. "With this sudden glitch, I'm concerned that diagnostics might not show up all malfunctions. I'll need you to conduct an on-site inspection of every comm station and hood on the *McKay*."

Yakata flinched on the inside. "Yes, sir. Right away, sir."

Captain Kinney was known for his swift and fitting discipline. Actually, she'd gotten off easy; she should have been the first on the deck, not counting those who were already there.

There was a sound beneath her feet. She stepped aside to clear the hatch. An acrid aroma preceded Dunn as he clambered to his post.

"Ah, very good." The captain's smile was not very pleasant, though his tone seemed to be. "Crewman Dunn will assist you."

Drive Section Service Module: 42.05.18 – 1700hrs

This was it. The final comm station on her half of the list. Yakata sighed as she pulled out the checklist and ran the last test. Carefully, she removed the housing then used her Fenix utility light and a telescoping mirror to visually inspect the wiring. After that she tested the connections. Finally, she closed the unit and toggled the activator.

"Dunn..."

"Go ahead..."

"Drive section comm inspection complete, how are you coming with the Engineering unit?"

"System's green to go." Dunn's voice remained even but Yakata detected an edge to it. It was barely perceptible, but his breath came out in quick, shallow huffs. She waited for him to report something catastrophic, but he remained silent.

"Okay, that's all of them. Wait for me at the main shaft." Yakata cut the link and toggled the activator again. "Command deck..."

"Go ahead." The captain's voice came through the relay sharp and precise. Yakata winced. He would remain on deck until she relieved him. That was part of what drove home the lesson. Her failure to follow orders affected everyone, right up to the captain, whom she respected more than anyone alive. Nothing, short of a fatality, would have made her feel worse about her lapse in protocol.

"On-site inspection of the communications system complete," Yakata responded, keeping her voice neutral.

"Acknowledged. I'll be waiting to hear your report."

"Yes, sir." Yakata groaned as she cut the link.

With haste, she secured her maintenance kit on her hip, slid the flashlight into its belt loop, and left the compartment. The sensors flanking the door registered her exit. The drive room went dark and the dim, stand-by lights of the causeway brightened. After nearly a decade of service, she generally took the lighting system for granted. Today she newly appreciated the comfort it represented. Even without the recent system's failure, Yakata was uneasy. Her nerves vibrated beneath the surface of her skin and her eyes ached from trying to penetrate the dark spaces around her. She'd yet to spy anything staring back. Her skin crawled though as she imagined a thousand pairs of eyes creeping forward into the now-darkened room behind her. Clenching her teeth, she cocked her head from side to side until the vertebrae ceased to pop. To her left, she thought she heard the faintest sound from somewhere near the pressurized tanks. Probably a loose valve. She made note of the section where she suspected the leak, and set off for the main shaft.

Dunn was not at the rendezvous.

Toggling the activator on her comm hood, the barest edge of anger sharpened her tone. "Crewman Dunn, report..."

Silence.

"Dunn, what is your location?"

Still no response.

What in the world was going on? Their personal comm hoods were the first to be tested. Both had operated fine. She went to the comm screen in the main shaft wall. With a couple of jabs she input the protocol that instructed the system to display the current location of all crewmembers.

She glanced down the list of names and locations: Captain Kinney and Crewman Suarez—Command deck; Crewmen Jackson and Chapman—Environmental Control Compartment; Specialist O'Neal —Temporary Science Lab; Crewmen Pittman, Jenks, and Gunter—Mess hall; and Crewman Dunn...

Port lateral airlock! Yakata powered down the display and set off back the way she came at a hard clip.

Bad enough they'd both drawn discipline duty, reporting back late would be impossible for the captain to gloss over this time. She tried her comm hood again, activating it with such force she could feel the surrounding fabric pull. "Crewman Dunn...respond..."

Nothing. She put on a little more speed through the shaft. A tight sensation took root in her gut. She tried again, "Come on, Dunn, talk to me. What's going on?"

No answer. The airlocks came into sight. Even in the dim light of the corridor, she could see a dark smear on the floor.

"Dunn! Damnit, Karl! Answer me!"

Yakata closed the last few meters. Dropping to one knee, she touched a finger to the slick spot. It came away bright red, the sweet, metallic tang unmistakable.

What happened? And where was Dunn? Sensors indicated the port airlock, but both chambers were dark. There should be lights. Lighting was automatic. She stepped to the side of the hatch portal and reached for her flashlight. The high-powered beam cut through the black pit beyond the glass.

Yakata gasped. For a second she could do nothing but stand there and stare at the horror revealed by the light: an EVA suit sprawled against the far wall, blood a solid curtain across the faceplate of the helmet.

A burst of static reminded her that the comm hood was still active, on stand-by. The sound snapped her out of the shock.

"Command deck..." She was surprised how low and calm her voice remained. The rest of her trembled. "Command deck, acknowledge...."

The only response was another burst of static.

She moved to the comm unit in the corridor wall and tried again. Again static hissed and crackled through the corridor, echoing through her comm hood. She moved back to the airlock door.

The beam of light glimmered on the helmet like sunlight through rubies. She could make out nothing beyond the faceplate. Swallowing hard, she swept the airlock with light as far as she could from side to side. Nothing. Not even more smears. No movement. Still, something did this. Yakata was acutely aware of the blind spots to either side of the hatch.

She punched in the sequence to open the airlock. The keypad didn't respond. She tightened her grip on the flashlight. It was awkward manipulating the manual release one-handed, but, with determination, she managed it. The hatch opened smoothly. Out wafted the heavy, copper-penny scent of blood and something else, something bitter and sharp. The lights still didn't engage.

"Dunn, can you respond?"

She peered into the room, her head just past the collar as she flashed the light into the corner to the right of the door. Nothing.

As she brought her light around to the other side, the comm hood gave a more energetic hiss. She flinched back at the unexpected sound. A blur of motion from the left caught her eye. Metal slammed against metal. From the shadows, hoarse breathing punched up into a roar. She now recognized the acrid odor in the air. She'd smelt it on the command deck, when Dunn came up the hatch.

There wasn't time to call out to him. There was only time to move. An industrial-grade spanner crashed into the airlock door just millimeters away from her head. Again, the weapon rose. She couldn't continue to evade; not in this restricted space. She brought the utility light up to block the spanner's descent and allowed her body to fall back upon the deck. The move cost her the light, which went spinning away, but her bones were intact.

She stared up into Dunn's face. He was barely recognizable. His eyes were wide and wild, a long, bloody scratch marred his face, and sweat stood out in hard beads on his forehead. The rest of him was coated in blood. He did not seem to recognize her. She watched as a tremor ran through his body. No matter what had passed between them, she didn't want to hurt him, not even to get away. She would, but she didn't want to. She prayed he came out of it.

"Dunn...Karl, what happened to you?"

She held her breath. For a moment, his pupils expanded. Recognition floated just beneath the surface. Then her comm hood hissed. His echoed in response. She had most of a second to watch him retreat behind the terror.

"Oh shit!" Yakata braced herself. This was going to hurt. Her only hope lay in the leverage of her position and her greater lower-body strength. The spanner came down full force. She dodged her torso as best she could, but took a glancing blow to her shoulder. Her left side went numb on impact. She wrapped herself around the spanner with her good arm and drew her legs up sharp. Snarling, she planted both feet in Dunn's gut and shoved for all she was worth.

The weapon remained in her possession, though it was close. Dunn went flying. Yakata winced as he crashed into the lockers, landing awkwardly on the sprawled EVA suit. She bit her lip at the fresh smear of blood across the dented metal. Bit harder against the impulse to go to him. Instead, she rolled to her feet and slammed the airlock hatch. Using the spanner, she wedged the door closed as best she could. It wouldn't hold long. She headed for the main shaft at a hard clip. Within the first five strides, the pain in her left arm triggered a grey haze across her vision. Gasping, she stopped running immediately.

Yakata blinked furiously, forcing herself to take slow, deep breaths, until the haze went away. Behind her she could hear banging, enraged and violent.

Gritting her teeth against the pain, she loosened her web belt and slipped the wrist of her damaged arm into the gap between belt and pants, angled across her stomach. She hissed with the pain and the sounds from the airlock increased in intensity.

She forced Dunn out of her thoughts and tightened the belt against her wrist, immobilizing the damaged arm as best she could. Once again, she set off, this time at a gentler, swinging lope. Her gut clenched. As she left the cacophony of the drive section behind, the faint sound of a warning klaxon could be heard elsewhere on the ship.

Yakata toggled her comm activator again. "Command deck... Come in, Captain Kinney." Not even a hiss sounded in her ear. "Deck officer, respond."

No answer; and her comm went dead, completely dead.

Abandoning her gentle pace, Yakata ran full out for the transport. The lift was slow, but one-handed, she would be even slower hauling herself up the ladder to the command deck. Her eyes locked on the lift mooring as it came into sight. The knots in her shoulders eased the slightest increment. The platform was there. She added another burst of speed.

Her steps faltered as she drew close. Something was not right. The lift wasn't seated properly in the track. It hovered about six inches off the mooring. She stopped where she was and tried to peer beneath it.

How had she missed the thin, crimson rivulets snaking across the deck? The fine, meandering tributaries flowing from the crushed body of Crewman Dave Jackson? Yakata fought the urge to be sick.

Was Dunn responsible? Was this why he wasn't at the rendezvous? Why he didn't answer her hails? Her throat spasmed and she had to swallow hard as she moved closer to examine the mechanism.

The body was tangled in the power couplings, bits of it pulped by the gears. Even if she could get the lift into motion, it would shred what was left of him. Only his face was untouched. His expression would haunt her.

A sound echoed up the corridor. Cursing, Yakata re-tightened her belt against her injured arm and climbed onto the lift. Her added force caused the platform to drop another inch. There was a sickening crack as something organic gave. She clenched her teeth and closed her eyes, emptied her mind of everything, and started up the lift. Before it had gone more than a few meters she slumped to her knees.

Central Shaft, Upper Utility Lift Mooring: 42.05.18 – 2100hrs

The lift locked into its upper mooring. Before her was the command deck hatch. She should get up. She had to report. The captain was waiting for them. Them. Not just her. Reality came rushing back. Yakata yanked herself to her feet with her good arm and gripped the ladder-track for balance. The hatch was open and the deck lights were at standby dim.

Every nerve in her body pricked. The command deck was unmanned. It was never unmanned. Leaning into the ladder, Yakata braced herself. She released her grip with her good hand and reached down into her maintenance kit. Near the bottom, she found the telescoping mirror she'd used earlier. Taking the reflective end carefully between her teeth, she angled the head and drew out the handle as far as it would go. She then edged the tool around the hatch. There were no bodies on the deck, and there were none walking around, either. Not that she could see, anyway.

The lights flared higher as she pulled herself through the hatch. She squinted against the sudden brilliance. It took a moment for her eyes to adjust. Closing the hatch, she keyed the lock with her personal code. Dunn wouldn't corner her again. Her shoulder throbbed in agreement. With a grimace, she settled into the command chair. Multiple warnings lit up the display in front of her. Alerts flashed over nearly every inch of the ship, a confusing dance of flood, fire, and vacuum. Sometimes all three at once in the same compartment. How much of it was real?

Clearing the screen, she prayed nothing would go critical before she could get this sorted out. She ran diagnostics, keying in commands one-handed. Half of the alerts disappeared. Next, she toggled the comm on the console. Nothing. Not even static. She had to try, though.

"Yakata to all crew, report." She set the hail to repeat and went back to diagnostics. It was halfway through and there were no major malfunctions yet. A host of minor ones, but those they could survive. Of course, that assumed the diagnostics system wasn't fried as well.

She then input the command to identify the locations of all on board, just as she had when she looked for Dunn. It took longer this time. The computer spit out multiple conflicting responses. There was no way to tell which one was accurate.

While she waited for diagnostics to complete, Yakata moved to the emergency kit. She selected an analgesic patch. After tearing it open with her teeth, she palmed it and slipped it past the collar of her coverall. It was cool, instantly soothing her battered shoulder. That taken care of, she settled back into the command chair.

Diagnostics was at ninety-five percent. Another alert went off as the logarithm completed. Yakata's eyes moved from the diagnostics display to the main console. It was the proximity warning. It shouldn't have gone off when they were under hyperdrive. She stood and went to the external monitoring station. Nothing appeared on the fore view. Yakata activated the aft cameras. Her finger trembled as she depressed the button. Her vision greyed out one moment, only to telescope into sharp focus the next. Something drifted by the lens out by the drive section, caught in the electromagnetic pocket of e'space surrounding the ship. Several somethings, in fact. Yakata swallowed against the acidic tang climbing her throat. Visions of her father's helmet overwhelmed her, eclipsing the images she didn't want to see. She distanced herself through extreme willpower and zoomed in on the debris.

"...all crew, report."

"Shit!" Yakata yelled as her own voice suddenly called out through both her comm hood and every speaker on the deck. Communications was back. She killed the auto repeat and sent out a fresh hail.

"Command deck to Captain Kinney..."

Her voice trailed off as she tweaked the settings on the monitor. The objects had come into focus. Her eyes slammed closed. But even with them tightly shut she could still see the empty gaze of Captain Kinney staring at her from the vacuum of space.

Personal Log Entry: 42.05.18 – 2230hrs, Dunn, K.
FUCK YOU! I don't know what you are, but I know what you're doing now, so fuck you! You made me hurt her. I would never hurt her. She is the only one who cares. Who still means something to me...

I know you can access what I'm writing here, because you knew how to mess with my head. Well access this: You will NEVER get me to hurt her again. You will never touch her again. I will destroy you!

Duty Log: 42.05.19 – 1230hrs, Yakata, U.
Reactor status – indeterminate;
O_2 levels – fluctuating;
Power – data unavailable.
Note: SC McKay operating under emergency conditions. Ship-wide malfunctions worsen. Member or members of the crew unstable. Captain Kinney; deceased, means unknown, body expelled from ship by unidentified personnel. At least three others likewise expelled, positive id cannot be made. Crewman Chapman; deceased, accidental or by design. Crewman Dunn; unstable, violent, temporarily restrained in port lateral airlock. Remainder of the crew; status unknown. First Officer Ushimi Yakata assuming command.

Out of habit, Yakata printed a hard copy of the duty log. Events must always be documented. Not that she expected anyone would ever read this account. As she tore the sheet from the printer, her eyes drifted across the page. She cursed and jerked her hand away. The page drifted to the deck, bold, black letters stared up at her:

They're all dead. You're all dead. Die already, bitch.

There was the faintest of sounds behind her. She whirled. O'Neal came through the hatch across the command deck, the one leading to the cargo bay and rendezvous station.

She took in the metallurgist's appearance: his coverall was torn, and dark stains across his chest glistened wetly. There was no sign he was the party injured. At his side, his prosthetic arm slowly flexed, as if the motion were unconscious. Yakata met O'Neal's gaze. She did not recognize the man staring back at her. His eyes were cold and hard, alien and bereft of humanity. His expression was neutral; as if she wouldn't notice something else lurked beneath. *There was so much wrong with this picture,* Yakata thought fleetingly.

"You plan to do what you're told?" he asked in a slow drawl, nodding toward the slip of acrylisheet on the floor.

His tone sounded as flat as his expression. Yakata's eyes flickered to the printout.

"I don't take orders from a piece of paper," she growled. "And I sure as hell don't take orders from you."

"We all have to answer to someone."

"Yeah, well the only person I answered to is drifting out by the engines," Yakata spat back at him. "Who do you answer to?" She moved to the side as she spoke, edging toward the hatch.

"You'll meet soon enough." The neutrality was gone. Pure evil crept through O'Neal's voice. He followed her movements like a raptor tracking prey.

Forget that, Yakata told herself. With the line of her body to block the action, she lowered her right hand back into her maintenance kit. Very carefully, she eased out her utility knife, her hand through the wrist strap and the hilt solid in her palm. She depressed the release button on the pommel and the blade silently deployed.

Yakata's muscles rippled beneath her skin. She braced herself, poised to react to whatever move O'Neal made. Her only real option was evasion. If he got a hold of her with that prosthetic, he would crush her before she could even flinch.

As the metallurgist advanced, a tremor went straight through Yakata's body. It took her a moment to realize it wasn't internal. She sucked in a sharp breath. Her gaze flickered away from O'Neal to the main display. Alert icons flashed, one by one. The system was losing power. Within moments they would no longer have enough to sustain hyperdrive. There was a boot dock just behind her and a tether up and to her right. She was going to need one of them shortly.

It would have to be the boot dock; she had too few functioning hands to grab a tether and use the knife. She edged herself closer. Let him think she was afraid of him; that she futilely distanced herself.

She was ready when the bottom dropped out of the universe. The ship shuddered as the electrogravitic drive envelope disintegrated. Simultaneously, she leaned back and jammed her heel into the dock. She was barely secure when there was a pop and a flash as intense as a hundred strobes going off right there in the room. Yakata squeezed her eyes shut just in time. From the heaving sounds, O'Neal had been caught unaware. She opened her eyes as reality righted itself in an orbital orientation. O'Neal floated in an uncontrolled sprawl on the far side of the command console. Around him floated globes of acrid vomit. As he bumped them, they burst into a dozen smaller globes, minus what clung to him. Feebly, his hand reached for the edge of the console.

Yakata grinned. In this state, he was no threat at all.

He groaned, and she laughed. She couldn't help it.

She went somber quickly, though, as hatred sharpened his gaze. The stench of malevolence overpowered the odor of bile. He looked ready to launch at her. Yakata tightened her grip on the utility knife. Let him try. He was a ground-pounder. Space was her element, and this was her ship.

There was a clunk and the manual release on the command deck hatch spun toward open. Yakata froze. Once she'd keyed the lock, even the manual release required her personal code to open the hatch. Only one person onboard had the slightest chance of figuring it out. Dunn.

Confusion infiltrated the evil glint in O'Neal's eye. She watched fury flood his expression as the hatch swung out. The open portal remained empty.

Yakata didn't relax. Now she had to be on her guard on two fronts, and her ex was no rookie in space. He must have been the one to disable the drive system. He certainly had the knowledge.

"Don't just stand there, 'Ta!"

Dunn peered around the edge of the hatch as he snapped at her. The scratch across his face had crusted over. His expression danced between violence and panic. She shifted her grip on the utility knife and turned her body so that her good arm could strike at either O'Neal or Dunn.

From the far side of the command console, O'Neal let out a serpentine hiss. She resisted the urge to turn to stare at him. Dunn represented the more potent threat at the moment.

She watched the muscles of his face clench and twitch in response to the sound O'Neal made. Dunn's breath quickened. The massive spanner he'd used earlier came into view. She braced herself, ready to yank her heel out of the dock the second she knew which direction to propel herself. But his attention wasn't on her. Dunn's eyes locked with O'Neal's. Yakata's gaze flickered from one to the other. Between them, they blocked the only ways out.

"Will you move it before he figures out how to get both of us!"

Yakata jumped, startled as Dunn spoke in rapid Japanese. She'd forgotten he knew her language. It wasn't something they'd used often. They both knew that O'Neal didn't share their knowledge. The entire crew was required to familiarize themselves with his profile before he came on board. She was surprised Dunn had enough of a grip on himself to use that intel.

"What...and I'm supposed to trust you over him?" She slashed back in the same tongue. "He's not the one who tried to cave in my head!"

"Just move it, 'Ta!" Dunn continued in Japanese. Sweat gleamed on his forehead and his eyes were wild.

Before she could dodge aside, he lunged. His free hand latched onto her belt. She snarled as he jerked her loose from the dock. Yakata gasped with pain, her damaged arm wrenched about by his handling. Her head spun at the sharp, sudden movement. Dunn angled her toward the hatch with practiced ease. At the same time, the hand gripping the spanner swung out, aimed at O'Neal's head.

There was a solid *thunk*: the sound of metal against flesh. Silence followed. Threat floated thick on the canned air. Yakata shifted her head to look back at O'Neal. His green eyes glowed with malice. She cursed and lost the thought as her quick glance took in his unbloodied head and Dunn's spanner caught by the metallurgist's flesh hand. Some oddly detached part of her brain wondered why he hadn't just grabbed it with the prosthetic.

Her answer was a strangled gasp from Dunn. With no visible effort, O'Neal's cybernetic limb crushed Dunn's wrist, the one holding the spanner.

The sight refocused Yakata's rage in an instant. She tried to wrench away from Karl's grip, throwing herself back as far as his tethering hold allowed to slash at his attacker with her utility knife. The tip sliced through O'Neal's shirt, barely scratching his shoulder. He did not even flinch.

Her curses cut off abruptly as Dunn shook her hard.

"Go! Now!" Karl snapped. Pain glimmered in his eyes, brilliant and jagged. Beneath that, he wordlessly pled with her. She stopped struggling, her brow drawn down in confusion.

Executing an effortless turn, she used the tip of her toe to propel herself off the overhead toward the hatch. She torpedoed through the opening, dropped the utility knife to hang by its strap, and caught the hatch collar with her good hand. Behind her a sick grinding sound filled the command deck.

She pivoted, catching sight of Dunn on his knees, his captured arm bent impossibly high behind his back. She growled and started to return to the command deck. She couldn't leave him to this.

"No! I said go! One of us has to get away...head for the Cans, now!" Despite his obvious pain, he continued speaking in Japanese. Yakata hissed in objection, but she dipped her head in a brief, sharp nod before pivoting around to zip down the main shaft. Behind her, she heard a loud snap as the sick sound of laughter drifted through the hatch. She had to fight the impulse to turn around and tear O'Neal to shreds.

"Yes...do run, little rabbit...I'll be along as soon as I'm done here. Shouldn't take long."

Yakata's blood thickened and her heart froze. O'Neal had just spoken to her in flawless, textbook Japanese.

An agonized scream came from the command deck. It rose sharply before an abrupt end.

Her good arm burned nearly as bad as her injured one. She ignored it and grabbed another rung of the ladder-track, slingshoting herself down the shaft. The echo of Dunn's final scream followed her. It filled her head until she heard nothing else. She tried to force the memory into the fading recesses where it belonged. It resisted.

The flickers of movement were back. The flashes of light behind her, just to the side of her vision. Halfway down the shaft it got to her. Growling deep in her throat, she turned to confront the phantoms that stalked her. A practiced flick of her wrist sent the utility knife back up into her grip and a moment's pressure deployed the blade. Her momentum sent her colliding with the substructure. The impact to her damaged arm sent true sparks across her vision, followed by a grey haze. She blinked it away and cursed.

The shaft behind her was empty. There was nothing behind her, and nowhere anyone might hide. She retracted the knife and let it drift at the end of its strap. With a little more care, she turned and continued to haul herself along, both arms throbbing as she went.

Her comm hood gave a sudden burst of static. Yakata jumped. Another growl filled her throat pulsing against her jaw. She nearly snatched the comm hood off to shred the delicate wiring.

"What the hell are you doing?!"

The unexpected outburst stayed her hand. Dunn. How...? Her gaze snapped to the command deck many stories above her head. She couldn't see him. He must be watching her on the monitors.

"I told you...to get out of here! Get to the Cans...now!" Dunn's voice was thin, strained.

"What happened to O'Neal?"

"Don't know...I passed out. He's not here." Sounds of movement filtered through the comm; rustling, a sharply drawn breath. What might have been a strangled sob...

"Dunn? Dunn!" Yakata's suspicions disintegrated beneath a fresh wave of concern.

"Don't yell, 'Ta." Karl's voice was low and weak. "You're making it hard to think.

"He left me for dead, which means he's after you."

"I don't understand what's going on here," she whispered.

"It's that damn artifact," he snapped back, but his voice quickly faded, slurring and losing focus. "None of this started until we salvaged that thing. It's screwing with our minds. It's screwing with the ship. Somehow it's infiltrated the system...and..." Static disrupted him in sharp bursts. "...anything electronic...nly use manual overr...only. Not malfunc...deliberate."

"The artifact! I have to get the artifact!"

"No!...amnit! Get the hell off this ship. Now!"

Immediately, uncertainty sank firm fingers into her thoughts. She had more reason to doubt Dunn than to trust him. And O'Neal had already proven their attempt at speaking covertly had failed.

"Move!"

No. Perhaps O'Neal left him for dead...or not. Dunn had attacked her once already. She couldn't help but wonder if this was a trap.

She would get her artifact, and then she was getting off this ship. It was foolhardy to continue to the airlocks, though. That's where they expected her to go. Besides, the Cans—as the escape pods were called by any spacer with experience—had precious little reserve, and almost no maneuverability. The distress signal was a joke. She wasn't ditching this ship just to suffocate slowly in space.

Like a swimmer doing laps, Yakata flipped end over end and hauled herself the way she'd come. The pods weren't the only option. There was that payload attached to the forward coupling, the inter-orbital shuttlecraft meant to transport Corporate bigwigs to their facilities surrounding Demeter. Even if O'Neal knew about it, he wouldn't expect her to try and escape that way. Transports were shipped dry, no fuel, no external tanks, and just enough juice to power the maneuvering thrusters and internals. Right now the shuttle was a big, floating box. But—most important for her— that big, floating box contained enough air to support seven adult males for fourteen days, without cracking the reserve tanks. That...and a state-of-the-art distress beacon.

All she had to do was reach it. Yakata renewed her efforts, keeping her eye on the reflectors as she went. No one threatened to come through the hatches ahead of her. As she neared the Temporary Science Lab, she again glanced both ways down the shaft.

Wherever O'Neal had gone, he wasn't stalking her.

Yakata opened the compartment and dove inside. She thanked God that the drive had not reengaged. The only blessing in this whole thing: weightlessness certainly made it easy to get around. Not to mention the obelisk would have been a dead weight if the ship were still under gravity.

Lights flared as Yakata slipped into the section where the artifact was stored. Immediately she noticed the door to the locker hung open, and nothing remained inside.

"No!" Yakata hissed with rage. She looked around, her gaze darting frantically, as if the obelisk might be sitting right in front of her. But it was useless. It was gone. She slammed the locker door and whirled, her anger taking over. The spectrometer still sat affixed to the table. It mocked her. She'd known O'Neal was out to screw her over. Her good hand snapped out, denting the housing of his costly machine. She let it fly again. It felt good. She took aim once more, until a reflection in the battered metal caught her eye.

O'Neal! She dove away from his raised fists, certain that any moment she would feel the crushing blow from his prosthetic. None fell. She twisted in midair, fighting to control her motions, to palm her knife and deploy the blade.

As she came to rest against the far bulkhead, Yakata felt a ripple of laughter seize her throat.

"What the hell?" she murmured aloud. The room was empty. No O'Neal hovered, ready to pummel her to pulp. Yet...

Yakata gripped her knife tighter and propelled herself toward the spectrometer. Had she truly lost it? Or was this proof of the sinister force Dunn claimed now possessed the ship? She tapped the dented surface with the tip of her utility knife. Tapped it right over the reflection of O'Neal. The micro image flinched back. Yakata giggled. It sounded jagged.

That was it then: she'd gone over the edge. She giggled again and chased the figmentary O'Neal around the spectrometer with rapid taps of her utility knife. She laughed full out and tasted salt drip over the rim of her lip onto her tongue. A sob slipped out next. The knife drifted down to its strap and she rested a gentle hand against the reflection.

"I'm sorry...I'm so sorry..."

She brought her face right up near the metal, noticing the terror on that tiny man's face. He wasn't looking at her, though; his gaze stared off into the room. It took her a moment to realize there were now two O'Neals trapped in the metal. Perhaps it was an accumulative thing: the longer she stared the more the image would multiply. Her next giggle bordered on a wail.

That was when the *ching* of flexing metal reached her ears. Her eyes went wide. She leaned against the machine. Clarity seeped back into her own reflection. The memory of the last time she and O'Neal had been in this room came to her. He'd taken the artifact out of the spectrometer and gone into painful convulsions. Her gaze snapped to the tiny O'Neal with the hazel eyes, somehow trapped within his own machine while something went around in his body. He gave the slightest nod. "I am sorry," she whispered as she snaked her hand around the housing.

With a mighty heave, she flung the machine at the O'Neal creeping up behind her, the one with something alien peering out of stormy green eyes.

Power couplings snapped. Metal collided with metal in a satisfying crunch. The creature's roar deafened her.

As she rocketed past, aiming for the hatch, she spared half a glance for her would-be attacker. The spectrometer drifted away from him. Massive bruises shadowed O'Neal's already dark shoulder. The prosthetic attached to it was crumpled, but the fingers flexed, if somewhat haltingly.

Her aim was off. She'd meant to cave in his head.

There was an odd gleam in O'Neal's eye as he locked gazes with her. She jerked her eyes away and maneuvered out of arm's reach.

She was nearly clear when he lurched up. His flesh hand shot out and grabbed her ankle. Screaming with rage, she flicked her wrist and palmed the dangling utility knife, the blade still deployed. She lashed out. The edge bit deep into the back of his hand.

She jerked the knife free and kicked out with her unfettered foot at O'Neal's still firm and bloodied grip on her ankle. He laughed up at her. The trapped O'Neal pounded furiously from the far side of his reflection; the evil one raised his battered prosthetic and caressed her calf with deceptive gentleness.

Frantic, Yakata tried to yank her foot free. She succeeded only in drawing him closer. Again the prosthetic stroked her leg, this time higher.

"Shh...It'll be okay..." he mocked.

Her vision went dark and flat. Nothing had depth or shading. Nothing was as crisply clear as his grip on her leg. Nothing mattered more than freeing herself from that hold. Without a second thought, she brought her knife around again and impaled O'Neal's hand...

...straight through to her ankle. More blood filled the room.

"Augh!"

O'Neal laughed over her scream as he tugged his hand away from the blade, bisecting his own flesh. The damage did nothing to hinder his movements. But for her, the motion sent shafts of breath-stopping pain shooting from her foot to the top of her head. The knife remained lodged in the muscle just above the ankle.

"Bad girl...you were supposed to head for the Cans."

Yakata whimpered. Clenching her teeth, she yanked out the blade, sending pearls of blood spinning through the bay. The strap went back over her wrist. The hilt locked in her grip. Again armed, she kicked off toward the hatch.

From just inside the room, O'Neal's laughter stole her breath. She waited for him to haul her back. She could already feel his fingers locked around her. Not again! She sent herself rocketing forward with reckless force. Her body careened off the interior walls. She slammed against the hatch collar with her bad shoulder. The injured foot snagged on the door. Agony nearly crippled her as her vision clouded and a buzz filled her ears.

It wasn't enough to drown out O'Neal as he called after her. "Run, little rabbit, run...it's so much fun to catch you."

Despite O'Neal's taunt, there were no sounds of pursuit. She had no illusion it would remain that way. Tumbling into the main shaft, Yakata planted her good foot against the track and shoved off, bulleting toward the nose of the ship. She cursed at the lights. Some sections activated as she passed, others went out, plunging her into darkness. She ignored it. After all her years on this ship, a little darkness wasn't going to screw her up.

As she neared the command deck there was a faint green ambient glow, like that given off by digital displays in the dark. It was impossible to make out if anyone was there. O'Neal was somewhere behind her, but what happened to Dunn? Intense sorrow gripped her heart as she remembered the last time she saw him. Yakata forced it away. He was either dead, or a danger to her.

Cautiously, she eased past the command hatch, keeping to the far side of the shaft. It was slow going, but she made it to the staging bay two levels up without incident. A glance behind her revealed no obvious motion, but her nerves vibrated with tension.

She turned back to the open hatch of the staging bay. The mechanism to seal the two-meter wide opening could close in less than thirty seconds. She released the knife and reached into her pouch for a spanner, wedging it into the grating where the retractable hatch was housed. It wouldn't hold long, but should another...malfunction occur, the obstruction would give her a little extra time to get clear.

Reaching just past the opening, she felt around for a tether bar to haul herself through. Something brushed against her hand in the darkness. She jerked back and palmed the knife, bracing herself for an attack. A whisper of sound taunted her ears. Her grip on the knife tightened even more, but nothing else came at her out of the dark. Yakata breathed out a growl.

Fine, she thought. *I'll do it the hard way.* She flung herself through the hatch, rocketing past the opening and deep into the bay, her body angled to intersect with the lift track. Instead, she collided with something soft and yielding. It was impossible not to scream as arms came around to encircle her.

No! She would not be caught so easily! Yakata brought up her knife and thrust brutally into the one blocking her way.

"'Ta..." The whisper was faint, and right by her ear. Yakata moaned and her knife hand jerked back. Warm globules bounced against her skin as the blade did more damage coming out than going in. The pinpoints of warmth sent her trembling.

No! Oh, God, no! Please no! Yakata's thoughts were frantic. She released the knife as if it were a contagion. Her now-empty hand scrambled around in her maintenance pouch as the knife bobbed on its strap. *Where was it? Where, damnit?* She forgot all about escape as she searched for her spare light among the jumbled tools. As her hand wrapped around it, and she depressed the button, a sudden clang from the direction of the hatch startled her. She fumbled the light. It made eerie arcs as it spun in the darkened bay, revealing small slices of her surroundings. Her gasp echoed through the compartment as the rotating beam briefly illuminated a blood-coated hand. Yakata lunged for the maintenance light. Before she could bring the beam around, there was a deep, rumbling chuckle behind her. She whirled and the main lights flared to life in the bay. She flinched and squinted against the sudden brilliance.

"My...and haven't you been busy?" O'Neal rested against the lift track, his arms crossed over his chest as he watched her. She noticed his gaze sweep the chamber. He frowned faintly as he looked right, but he made no move toward her or the room.

The last thing she should do was take her eyes off him. The impulse, however, was irresistible. Yakata pivoted until she could see the whole of the bay.

The blood rushed from her head. She barely heard O'Neal's malicious laughter. Around her floated three bodies. Her unaccounted-for crewmen... She immediately recognized the one to the right as Dunn, much bloodier, but still clearly him. The closest to her, however, was John Pittman. From his gut streamed a trail of ruby-red bubbles.

She was overcome by the urge to fling the utility knife from her, only that would have cut her probability of survival down even lower. It was an effort to tug her eyes away, to get past the horror. She told herself he was already dead. Beyond Pittman floated Anita Suarez, her expression softer, more feminine in death than it had ever been in life. Old spacer that she was, she looked like a frightened child now. A frightened child frozen in intense and unbearable pain.

Yakata refused to look more closely at Dunn.

She cursed and turned on O'Neal once more, her knife in her hand, though she didn't remember flicking it up. O'Neal continued to laugh.

"'Ta...no...."

Again, the bodiless whisper by her ear. No...from her comm hood! Only Dunn ever call her 'Ta. She glanced sideways, trying to catch the subtle motion breathing alone would have caused. It was so hard to tell at this angle.

"Damn it, 'Ta, come...get this thing..." The strained whisper was no product of her imagination. He 'drifted' ever so slightly; just enough to reveal the outline of a line-gun hidden in the curve of his body. Behind him she could see the half-open storage locker the tool had come from.

Without another thought, she braced both legs against the wall. Pain rippled from her ankle, but she needed equal force to keep herself headed straight as she launched herself forward. O'Neal arrowed toward Dunn, as well, but Yakata was closer.

Grasping the gun and using her momentum to pivot the rest of her mass, she braced the improvised weapon against her body and jerked the release.

There was a *whoosh* and a *thud*. O'Neal went rocketing across the bay toward the opposite wall. His head slammed into the hull and then the only motion was his body recoiling from the impact.

Numbness set in. *Could that be it? Was it that simple?* she thought as she drifted where she was, the gun still gripped in her hand. Beside her, Dunn moaned and it barely reached where her psyche had retreated.

The steady tug on the rope, though...that went right to her nerve centers.

"Oh, shit!" She let go of the line-gun and wrapped her good hand in Dunn's vest.

"N-no...you have to survive," he murmured, batting away her hand. "Can't do that hauling my ass behind you."

"Bullshit!" she growled. "You made it this far, I'm not leaving you here to die."

"I'm...I'm d-dead, either way."

She ignored his failing whisper, and pushed off, sending them past the bodies. Her mind shut down as she did so, focused on one goal: freedom. Nothing existed but the nose dock of the *McKay* and the payload it led to.

And suddenly, they were there.

She let go of Dunn's vest to work the manual release. The hatch clanged open and she reached for Dunn once more. He gripped her hand back. He trembled violently. She turned to look at him, to gauge how much distress he was in.

"No!" she shouted, as she spied O'Neal past Dunn's shoulder, raising the retracted line-gun. But it was too late. She felt the impact as the hook embedded itself in Karl's back. "No...no..." she sobbed. Not Dunn. Not when she... "No...I l-love you! No!"

Tears streamed down her face as she watched the awareness fade from his eyes. *No.* But this protest was silent, weak. *Does it matter now,* she wondered, *if I get away?* But the tug of the line decided her. She roared with rage and yanked back. O'Neal and whatever rode him would not have Dunn.

She brought up her utility knife and severed the line. Grabbing Karl's vest, she tugged him through the forward airlock. He bobbed behind her as she cycled the hatch. Yakata was numb as she took them through the yacht access. She gave him a gentle nudge to send him drifting deeper into the cabin as her hand danced automatically through the manual release sequence for the docking ring.

As they separated from the *McKay*, she could swear she heard the ghost of O'Neal's laughter.

She dropped into the command chair of the luxury yacht, barely noticing the sensual caress of fine doeskin leather. Her only concern was powering up the systems. Lighting and atmospherics engaged, followed by the exterior cameras.

The numbness faded as she realized how near Demeter they were. There was hope of rescue. A solid chance for survival. Her hand hovered over the distress beacon, but drew back, leaving the unit inactivated. Why bother? Dunn was gone.

"No...you must survive."

Yakata shivered as Dunn's earlier words whispered through her thoughts. Clenching her eyes against the heartache, she brought her hand back and slammed it down on the distress beacon button.

Rescue would come now. And she would have to go on. Alone.

As that realization hit her, she watched the *McKay* fire its engines. She deftly manipulated the contoured joystick controlling the external camera, panning it in the ship's wake.

What is he up to now? she wondered, unable to turn away. The *McKay* angled further to the left and the display in front of her blazed fiercely, blinding her a moment. The system adjusted the filters until the brilliant sun was no more than a distant, glowing disk marred only by a rapidly diminishing black speck.

"Enjoying the show, Ms. Ushimi?"

Yakata jerked as O'Neal's voice came over the yacht's speakers. She cursed herself for forgetting to disengage the remote sensors connecting the two ships.

"Why?" she hissed.

"Where's the terror," he purred, "if there's no one left to know exactly how fucked you all are?

"Oh yes, and thanks for the ride."

As his words faded, the yacht's lights flickered out, plunging Yakata into darkness. She fumbled with the control panel, frantically trying to reengage them, to no avail. Her only illumination was the display in front of her.

She couldn't hold back a whimper. She was no longer comfortable with the dark. O'Neal's disembodied laugh wrapped around her just before he closed the link. She was so shocked it took a moment for her to realize the *McKay's* hyperdrive had engaged.

Horrified, she watched the ship's graceful arc; the shimmer of its electrogravitic drive envelope mesmerized her. Yakata held her breath. She could still see the glittering trail streaming behind the transport, but knew it had, in fact, already plunged into the sun. Eight minutes later, the sunlight contracted, the glowing ball getting smaller and smaller.

O'Neal's voice echoed in her head. An old memory from when he had still been himself and the spectrometer had fed them an impossible reading on the obelisk: *It's as if the artifact absorbed the light.*

She shuddered and watched as the star died, its fire eaten up by an ancient evil no larger than her head.

Yakata found herself in complete darkness with her dead.

Dunn. The spaced crew. In her panicked mind, she pictured each of them in a mask of her father's face.

Her breath came in rapid huffs and her body shook until she had to grip the console to remain in the chair.

How long before we all die? she thought, staring in the direction of Demeter, an entire planet suddenly and inexplicably plunged into bitter-cold darkness.

The comm hood crackled and Yakata's heart seized.

"Yummy," O'Neal's voice whispered malevolently in her ear. "Want to come get us? We'll do dessert..."

Yakata screamed.

Unit Patch of the
42nd Rapid Deplayment Squadron,
Allied Forces Starfleet

The universe is harsh and unforgiving, especially during wartime. This is particularly hard on the civilians caught in the crossfire. But even in the midst of such chaos, there will always be those that serve as guardians against the inevitable cruelties of war. Those who feel their job is to protect the innocent, no matter the cost.

Greg Schauer

SHEEPDOG

Mike McPhail

"Most of the people in our society are sheep. They are kind, gentle, productive creatures who can only hurt one another by accident. Then there are the wolves, and the wolves feed on the sheep without mercy. Then there are sheepdogs, and I'm a sheepdog. I live to protect the flock and confront the wolves."

Paraphrased from "Sheep, Wolves, and Sheepdogs"
Lt. Col. Dave Grossman

IT WAS A RELIEF TO FINALLY ESCAPE THE SMOTHERING DARKNESS OF THE OLD-GROWTH forest. Its ancient canopy had long ago meshed to form an impenetrable barrier blocking the life-giving light of this world's sun, Tau Ceti. Nature had not seen fit to give the planet a celestial traveling companion, as with Earth and her moon, so the term 'the dark of night' had a whole new meaning here.

As starlight shown on the scene through towering grasses at the edge of the tree line, the suit's all-governing computer, or Pacscomp, powered down the peripheral, infrared lamps, once again allowing the helmet-mounted, electro-optical scopes to gather the faint ambient light and amplify it into a false-color day.

The armor-clad figure pressed forward until the sea of grass parted like waves breaking against the bow of a ship. Visibility was less than a few inches, fostering a complex feeling of concealed safety and overt vulnerability as his passage created a hole in the surrounding landscape.

Navigating by landmarks was impossible, yet the scouts pressed on, guided only by the down-view overlay, which gave them an approximation of their position. As with all things deemed vital to the cause, both sides in the conflict had electronically fought for control of the orbiting constellation of LandNav satellites, ultimately rendering the system virtually useless. So it was the suit's digital compass, in sync with the transponder they had set up back at the insertion point that guided them this night.

"Slow it down," another spoke directly into his mind, the tone was flavored by the adrenaline-fueled tension of the moment.

The scouts had been moving at a trot since leaving the bushes at the edge of the tree line. Without responding, the one in the lead down-shifted into a walk and focused on the map. Its scale indicated that they were about twenty yards from the parameter roadway, heading straight for a rock outcropping.

The sound of his breath opening and closing the suit's air handling system was almost drowned out by the background noise of the winds dancing across the field, whipping the grasses, and creating a white nose reminiscent of falling rain.

Glancing over toward his comrade, there—superimposed against the wall of foliage—was a green, rounded-point triangle, topped with the letters RWL. Its relative size indicated that the scout was less than five yards away. The sight of his teammate's icon was reassuring; it added a physical presence beyond just the comm traffic, and the voices in his head.

"I'm telling you," his comrade continued the conversation they'd started earlier, *"she was up all day and night screaming and demanding my attentions."* A feeling of being tired washed across the electronic commune.

"And…?" asked Ke'Se, trying to keep his amusement from being conveyed.

"And so I did as nature intended," replied Ra'Ewl with a hint of pride. *"But in truth, there's only so much enthusiasm before all that biting and scratching gets old."*

"You're a spaz for complaining," responded Ke'Se. *"So, no nap then?"*

The very top of the rock outcropping came into view, less as an image, and more of a void punched out of the starry sky.

"Just what we had on the flight in." Ra'Ewl slowed and then took up a position at the foot of the rock. Its surface was almost weathered smooth, but at least this facing sloped up to its summit at a traversable angle.

"Going right," stated Ke'Se as he crouched for a slow pass along the side of the rock. Now just a yard from the cleared edge of the grasses, he

went down onto his belly. He spied the world through the last few inches of cover.

"Clear?" asked Ra'Ewl impatiently as he revved up for the leap.

"Standby." Ke'Se crawled forward and gently pushed his head through the grass, opening up the field of view to his helmet-mounted scope. To his front was a swath of crushed stones that had been used to stabilize and defoliate the ground around the roadway. With a slow pan of his head, he scanned the area for any immediate threats.

"You're good to go."

"Going up," Ra'Ewl communed with an accompanying *hooff* over the comm as he leaped. The jump brought him to just below the grass tops. Gaining purchase on the rock took a little more than just the traction pads on his boots. With a snap he deployed the fighting claws, and pressed hard against his toes. At a measured pace—as laid down by eons of evolution— he moved slowly toward the crest.

Feeling more like a gecko climbing out onto a rock to sun himself than a predator on the hunt, Ra'Ewl settled onto the high point and waited for the suit's equivalent of chromatophores to shift into a dark gray. *"I AM...the rock,"* he communed with a sense of playfulness.

After another quick sweep, Ke'Se pivoted to look up at Ra'Ewl, whose green icon floated ethereally at the back of his helmet. Despite the carapace plates that made him look like a child's toy robot, there was still no mistaking that he was fifteen pounds worth of cat, stuffed into AS'Is (Allied Standard Issue) body armor.

Although spawned from a thousand generations of domestic house cats, nature was no longer in the driver's seat. As the end product of the animal- experimentation phase for the Synaptic Interface—direct mind– machine communications, or commune—Doctor Jonathan Parr's feline lab rats took on an unexpected life of their own, as comrade-in-arms with their bygone tormentors.

From his perch, Ra'Ewl could see the town's parameter roadway, with its long, curving arc and accompanying sidewalk. There were no lights to be seen, only the myriad of road-designating phosphorescent reflectors giving up their stored energy to the night.

The town of Stratford was typical for Demeter, a bullseye layout with a series of concentric circular roadways and spoke avenues, dividing up lots. At its apex was the Administrative Centre, which housed everything that an isolated town of two thousand projected residents might need.

"Raul what is your position?" came over the comm in a slight Scottish accent.

Ra'Ewl's tail twitched at the thought of making mischief. "Standing on a rock," he replied over the comm via the commune, and then turned to look down at his fellow scout.

There was a pause. "Aye. Echo status?" replied the voice from his helmet's speakers, asking if they had spotted any sign of the enemy, or Echo, from the phonetic alphabet.

"Still looking for those bad-guys." Both he and Ke'Se started to chirp with laughter.

Yet another pause. "Raul. Kizzy. Maintain comm procedures," instructed the voice. The letters OWN shown on the squad-ban display.

Ra'Ewl did a quick front stretch, and then reared up into a sitting position, all the time scanning for movement.

This isn't the first time Corporal Owens has expected us to play like soldiers, thought Ra'Ewl to himself. Being an expatriate of the Dominion, only Owens knew why he'd chosen to fight under Allied Military authority.

"Owens, the bad-guys can't pick up our comm traffic, and even if they could, they don't have the Pacscomp to translate it. That's why they're all hot-and-heavy to try and get their hands on one."

"Aye, I've been told all that, but I'm sure Donitz felt the same way about Enigma," quipped Owens. "So if you two are through pissing about, I need you to move onto the objective."

"Who's Donuts?" asked Ke'Se.

"Haven't a clue." Ra'Ewl leaped from the rock. *"On the move."*

The outermost ringed streets of Stratford were nothing more than a flattened bit of land, with yellow boundary lines and brass benchmarks proclaiming their future address. Many of the lots already had their poured foundation slabs and adjoining utilities trenches running out to the street. Just ahead, a picket of landscaping trees marked the boundary to the completed section of the town.

Ra'Ewl swung left at a trot, following the tree line with Ke'Se in tow. Through the thicket of screening foliage laid the boxy, two-story prefab buildings that were predominately used across the planet. No doubt each had been adorned by their owners to express their own personal idioms, but here in the dark they were just more oppressive, monolithic structures seemingly devoid of life.

"Ra'Ewl!" communed Ke'Se, with a sense of discovery.

The Parr looked back toward the construction zone. One of the slabs had a large piece missing next to a wide depression. As they approached, the ground they covered was awash in a spray of dirt and shattered bits of concrete.

"This is it?" asked Ke'Se.

Ra'Ewl had already turned and was looking about for others. *"Yeah I think so; it looks like two more over this way,"* he replied before heading off.

It took them a few minutes to arrive at the third hole; this one was in a patch of open ground. Ra'Ewl estimated that the crater was about two and a half yards across and a foot deep. He then noticed that Ke'Se wasn't looking at the crater, but back toward the house.

Ke'Se purred with fascination at a tree between him and the building. To say the tree was broken would have been an understatement. The crown had been blown off, leaving foot-long splinters sticking up at odd angles. The upper portion now sat on the ground, resting against the bole of the tree.

"Fell short," commented Ke'Se as he moved in for a closer look.

Ra'Ewl suddenly felt the need to get to higher ground, but the best he could do was a nearby pallet of building materials. It was piled high with polymer sacks, many of which were torn open and had hemorrhaged their contents. They were filled with some form of granular material. With a dash and a leap he landed on top and gave a good hard look about.

"Owens, from Ra'Ewl," he communed; now watching Ke'Se as he moved behind the devastated tree, to be replaced by just his floating icon.

"Owens, go ahead, Raul." the letters OWN brighten on the Parr's display.

"We're on station. Negative contacts. There are three confirmed hits and a possible tree burst. The craters are the right size for the enemy's eighty-ones." he reported.

"Understood, what did they hit?"

Ra'Ewl had another quick look. "Nothing. They landed in the construction zone back behind the first street of houses." Ke'Se's icon was receding, heading off toward the nearby house. Ra'Ewl was anxious to join him.

"Roger that."

Ra'Ewl leaped from the pallet and darted off. "Owens, we say 'acknowledged' in this cat's Army," he communed, knowing that it would annoy Owens to be caught making such a simple mistake.

"Acknowledged," the human said in a taut tone. "Keep me informed. ETA about fifteen minutes, Owens out."

As Ra'Ewl cleared the trees, he saw that Ke'Se had crossed the backyard and was now just outside the building. Crouched down, he used the thickness of the back deck for cover. The storm door's clear, polycarbonate panels were fractured, and the inner door lay open and at an angle.

Ke'Se briefly looked over as Ra'Ewl settled in next to him. *"I'm getting a glow on thermal from somewhere near to front,"* reported Ke'Se. His display was showing him the world from his scope's far-infrared pickups. Everything was painted in shades of cold blue to white hot; the interior of the house was awash in warm colors reflected off numerous surfaces; it looked very much like a room lit by a fireplace.

"Big or little?" asked Ra'Ewl, as he slowly moved off toward the left side of the house.

Ke'Se checked the color-coded thermal key at the bottom of his display. *"Maybe around eighty degrees ambient, it's hard to tell without line of sight. Whatever it is, it's small."* he added.

"Like a monkey-boy has his helmet off?" Ra'Ewl was now just under a large picture window that faced out onto what appeared to be the home-owner's garden project. The cleared ground was edged with a continuous strip of black plastic, while underneath the window lay a neatly stacked pile of rock pavers.

"I don't think so; it's bigger than that."

Checking that the pavers screened him from the street, Ra'Ewl stretched up his full length; he was just short of being able to look into the window. *"Okay, be ready to run if someone spots me,"* he communed, almost excited by the possibility.

"Acknowledged." Ke'Se backed up so he could get a running start into his turn.

"Suit, scope up," Ra'Ewl commanded. A small insert window opened on his display. Its round image was almost fish-eyed, and clearly in motion. At the end of its extension, the flexible scope stood a foot over his head, and parroted the movements of the helmet.

The space was a living room, decorated in a modular, out-of-the-catalog style, with two couches forming an L near the window. Across the room was a theater display, its flat-panel screen gouged, the frame missing pieces.

Tilting his head, he scanned the area along the floor in front of the seating area. There, partially covered by the far edge of the couch, sat a child, it was doubled over as if resting its head on its knees.

"Shit!" communed Ra'Ewl conveying a feeling of annoyance.

"Big shit or little shit?" misconstrued Ke'Se. Ra'Ewl ignored his attempt at being a smartass.

"Suit, scope down." The scout was on the move even before the scope locked safe into its housing. *"Back door, we're going in."*

Ke'Se was standing to one side as Ra'Ewl reached the storm door. Standing up on his hind legs and grabbing the knob with both paws, Ra'Ewl gave it a twist and reared back. As the door gapped, Ke'Se intervened and shoved it open with his body.

Cautiously, Ke'Se peered around the edge of the inner door. Nothing had changed. They entered the room slowly; its floor was covered in rough tiles and was lined with counter tops and appliances. To the right was a staircase.

"Check the second floor," ordered Ra'Ewl.

As Ke'Se went for the stairs, the hot spot came into view through a myriad of chair and table legs.

Ra'Ewl could feel his comrade's concern. *"Go check for bad-guys,"* he ordered.

Quietly Ke'Se climbed the stairs as Ra'Ewl lowered himself into a stalk, and moved to get a better look. It seemed that he had been too distracted by the sight of the child to see the truth of the situation. Lying there, just on the other side of the dining room table separating the living room from the kitchen, was a body. Ra'Ewl didn't bother with a biometric scan, if the human had been among the living Ke'Se would have seen that on thermal. *"Anything?"*

"Negative. On the move."

Ra'Ewl stood up and walked toward the child, swinging wide to avoid the body and the pool of congealed blood that surrounded it. Looking back he could see that Ke'Se had just turned the corner.

Together they stood in silence and pondered the scene. The child was a small female, dressed in a long-sleeved T-shirt and overalls. Her head rested forward against her knees, and her long hair draped to the sides of her black, rubberized field boots. One arm was up underneath her, holding some form of plush animal, while the other hung down; its hand was gripping the hair of the adult. It too was female.

"Suit, thermal disengage." He turned to face Ra'Ewl. *"Mom?"*

Ra'Ewl didn't answer what he felt was obvious. *Things are getting complicated*, he thought to himself, as he looked around in the hope that an answer to this problem would just materialize if he looked hard enough.

In a sense it did; while he was distracted, Ke'Se had moved to within just a foot of the girl and was reaching out to touch her leg.

"No stop that, bad Parr, don't..."

Ke'Se had stopped as Ra'Ewl barked the order, but with paw outstretched, the scout stood frozen in the moment as the girl looked up. Her eyes were dilated against the darkness, and through his night vision scopes they shown as bright as a cat's. There was just a momentary pause, as confusion washed across the girl's tear-stained face and her young mind raced for an answer.

He had just lowered his arm when tremors shook her body, and the girl screamed. Involuntary he leapt, flinging himself back almost a yard. Ke'Se landed with a padded thump, back arched. The comm was now awash with primitive emotions, as the sounds of his hissing and growling flooded the channel.

Ra'Ewl fought to maintain his composure. *"Ke'Se, stand down!"* he ordered, while trying to drive across the feeling of being in control.

Ke'Se wound down as he watched the girl desperately trying to backpedal away from him, only to be stopped by the edge of the couch.

"Just great, get over here," demanded Ra'Ewl; the girl's voice was strained, as if she'd already given as much as she could to the effort. No longer screaming, she trembled with fear, while clutching her stuffed animal.

As Ke'Se moved passed Ra'Ewl, he pressed himself against his comrade's side asking for forgiveness, resulting in a series of thumps as composite plates smacked into each other.

"What were you thinking?" The tip of Ra'Ewl's tail flicked with annoyance.

The image of sitting on the floor and playing with his friend's children hung in Ke'Se's mind. *"Mac's kids always liked it when I patted them,"* Ke'Se communed defensively. In the early days of the Project, Dr. Parr had isolated and switched off the gene that created the cat's claws, making his front paws more like prehensile hands, than weapons, and thus safe for playing with children.

"Yeah, but here and now, all you are is a Jonathan-forsaken monster; just a shadow against the dark." Ra'Ewl paused, as if hearing his own words being spoken by someone else. *"Get out of your suit,"* he ordered.

"What? Are you spazzed?" The very thought clearly panicked Ke'Se.

"Just do it." Ra'Ewl looked around to see how much cover they had. The windows had no blinds or curtains, so they must have been the type that electronically went opaque.

"Why me?" argued Ke'Se, as he assumed the position.

Ra'Ewl looked for the main controls; odds were they were somewhere near the master's seat on the couch across from the theater display. He moved with all the stealth he could muster, while watching the girl and hoping that he didn't frighten her any more than he already had. *"Because, the monkey-boys gave me an AS'ls hair cut to deal with the suit's tactile contact points, whereas you are still fuzzy,"* he communed with a sense of amusement over his partner's growing distress.

Lying on his stomach, Ke'Se moved his front paws to either side of his helmet. With a firm push, he depressed the twin latches; the backpack portion of his armor popped opened. Arching his back, he pulled his head free, leaving his helmet still connected to the suit's neck coupling.

Over the commune, a wave of disgust hit Ra'Ewl, who was almost to the couch. Turning so he could see Ke'Se's head, but his ears were back and he had one paw over his nose, as he had seen the humans do in such a situation. *"The smell..."* Ke'Se trailed off.

"Deal with it; we'll have a Vettech give you a bath when we get home." At the moment the girl was distracted by the sounds of Ke'Se extracting himself from his armor. Ra'Ewl leapt for the couch; there, built into the padded armrest, was the controller. With a stubbly digit he pressed the window-screen button. In an instant, the stars no long shown through the panels, as the dark became black. The girl gasped in horror and started sobbing.

"The batteries still work," he mused as he turned to face the scene. Ke'Se was out of his suit and standing in front of the child. *"Ready?"* Ra'Ewl asked, before realizing his mistake. The Pacscomp could only communicate with the user's Synaptic Interface within the confines of the helmet.

"Suit, external," he instructed. "Hi there." sounded the male-neutral voice from the Parr's external speakers. The girl turned toward the voice, her eyes wide; her mouth hung open as she panted to breathe.

"It's okay, we're here to help. Don't be scared." It sounded cliché. *"Suit hold, lights, thirty-percent, maximum diffusion, engage."* The helmet's side lamp came on. Even at its low setting it still came on like a blazing sun. Ra'Ewl's night vision switched off.

The girl squealed and raised her arms to cover her eyes against the light, the blue plush animal she had been holding dangled precariously by its long ears; a trail of white stuffing leaked from its midsection.

Ke'Se had guessed his comrade's intentions and was prepared. Slowly, he opened his eyes, allowing his pupils time to constrict. The girl's boots stood like a grime-splattered wall in front of him. Not wanting a repeat of her earlier reaction, he decided not to reach for her, instead he purred.

Timidly the girl peered around her arms in search of the sound. Her blue eyes locked onto Ke'Se's, who then squinted his eyes in greeting and tipped his head slightly to one side to be cute.

For the first time something less then terror shown on the girl's face; slowly she unfolded herself, and tentatively reached out toward the black and white cat. Ke'Se stepped forward, thrusting his head under the girl's hand and pressed into her palm.

To Ke'Se surprise, the girl giggled nervously and rocked forward onto her knees to throw her arms around him in an effort to pick him up. Of course, at fifteen pounds he was easily over a third of her weight, so he just stood there, as she hugged him and buried her face into his soft fur.

"Raul from Owens, status!" came in over the comm. "What's happened to Kizzy?"

Ra'Ewl paused for a moment to figure out what to say; no doubt Ke'Se's icon fell of the grid once he was out of range of his Pacscomp. "Ah, we have a domestic situation here," he answered.

"Be more specific."

"We found a child in the house near the tree strike," he replied, wondering what would happen next. Looking up, he could see Owens' icon in the distance.

"Standby. I'll be with you shortly," he instructed.

Sighting in on the scouts' icons, Owens entered the building, closing the damaged door behind him as best he could. The Parr's small helmet lamps lit up the house as if it were high noon. Owens went down on one knee, using the counters for cover from the windows; his weapon was at the ready. "Raul, turn them off." The house went black; the intensity of his night vision display rose to compensate. The false safety of the darkness returned.

Staying low, Owens moved over to the body. Next to it, the girl had reared back trying to take Ke'Se with her. The Parr—now standing up on his back legs—was held tight as if he was the girl's only hope. Lowering his weapon, Owens allowed it to hang across his chest by its strap.

"Raul?" he commed, as he reached for the body. Firmly he grabbed it by the shoulder and moved it; it was cold and sluggish, but not stiff. *Whoever she was, she's been dead for more than a day*, he surmised.

"Raul..." he repeated, when he realized that the Parr was sitting next to him. "Did you check their RF tags?" he asked, looking over at the girl. A knot now gripped his stomach. He'd seen that look of terror before, and not on the faces of a stranger, but of a friend, long ago, when her own parents had met a similar fate.

"Negative, I don't have a reader," communed Ra'Ewl, as his suit's synthetic voice joined in.

With a practiced hand, Owens reached into his side pack and retrieved a wallet-sized device. He then held it near the body. "Suit, RF scan." With that command, an ID photo and data line appeared with an arrow pointing at the body. Her name is—was—Sherilyn Carter; it went on to list that she was married and had a daughter.

Owens then aimed the reader at the girl. "Christine 'Crissy' Carter," he read aloud over the comm; "Year of birth, 2059. She's only three." Owens fought to keep his emotions in check.

"Did you find anyone else?" he asked, wondering about the father.

"Nope."

Owens gently reached over and put his hand on Mrs. Carter. Silently he prayed. He then took a deep breath; it cleared his mind and helped steady his emotions.

He then reach into his pack and pulled out a disposable chemlight. Removing the safety cap, he depressed the igniter, which popped. As the chemicals mixed, the room became awash in a soft white glow.

"Sheeet." meowed Ke'Se in Purrsing, the closest thing the Parr had to a spoken language, as Crissy clutched him in a death grip when Owens was revealed by the light. Clad in his AS'Is carapace armor, the soldier must have looked like some form of unimaginably large insect, suddenly materializing out of the darkness. Crissy was frozen in fear.

"It's okay, he's not going to hurt you, he's a friend." said Ra'Ewl in an effort to comfort the girl.

"Easy, easy..." Owens commed before realizing she could not hear him. "Suit, external." "Easy there, Sweetie," he said, calmly leaning forward, and motioning with his hand. Clearly it wasn't working. Owens was still some faceless monster in her eyes.

"Suit, unlock." he said as he reached up and pulled the mandible portion of his helmet free. In response, the visor raised, leaving his face framed by his comhood. "It's okay, Sweetie, please don't squish the cat. They're expensive," he said gently.

Ke'Se's tail swished with annoyance at the remark, but at least the girl calmed down.

"Raul, you get Kizzy back into armor," Owens said as he stood up and walked toward the kitchen, then up the stairs.

There was no sign that the girl was going to give him up. Ra'Ewl knew Ke'Se could fight his way free, but the scout would never consider doing so, even as a last option. Longingly, he turned to see what his comrade was up to.

Ra'Ewl was now next to them reaching for the girl's discarded plushy; his glove's prosthetic grippers were deployed and acting as a set of opposable thumbs. With the toy in paw, he moved off in a three-legged hop, to sit down with his back toward the two.

Owens had returned; his helmet was closed with the visor still up. He was carrying a small blanket adorned with wide-eyed blue bunnies. "What's the hold up?"

"Working on it," Ra'Ewl said. Turning he held up the plushy as he closed his medpack; the rabbit's torn abdomen was now covered by a gray contact bandage. He gently shook it, making its long ears flop about.

"It's okay, Sweetie, you can take your rabbit," Owens assured her.

Reluctantly, she let go of Ke'Se and grabbed for the toy. She clutched it even tighter than she had the cat, all the while giving Owens and Ra'Ewl a pouting frown, as if their handling of her toy was more of an offense than their presence. Ke'Se backed away the moment she took possession of the plushy.

"Right," Owens said in a firm tone. "We're going to EVAC her to the recovery site."

"What about the mission?" asked Ra'Ewl, as he helping Ke'Se back into his armor. "Couldn't we just leave her here, and pick her up on the way out?"

Owens knelt in front of her; setting the blanket aside he reached over and placed his hands on her upper arms. "Can't take the chance. If something happened..." he trailed off. "Besides, we've accomplished the primary objective, so everything else is 'up to the discretion of the team'," he quoted.

"What if we leave Ke'Se here to keep an eye on her?"

Ke'Se was mostly back into his suit, with only his head still sticking out. "Feek que," he meowed, and pushed his head down through the neck coupling. Ra'Ewl then flipped his backpack closed, and like a man doing CPR, he pressed down onto his comrade's back with both paws, throwing his weight into the effort.

"On line," communed Ke'Se, as he flipped his head around while trying to get his paw up to his faceplate as if trying to groom. *"Damn, I stink."*

Owens angled his head, both Parrs' icons shown on his display. "You two, outside, check for Echoes," he ordered.

Ke'Se tromped off in compliance; Ra'Ewl sat down next to Owens. "You know she's going to shine like a marker beacon in the infrared."

"No shite," Owens agreed. "All we can do is dampen her down, and break up her silhouette."

"What about telling...someone she's here?" said Ra'Ewl reluctantly; he'd expected Owens to spaz out on him for even suggesting turning her over to the bad guys; the Legion.

"That's not happening, cat," stated Owens, a determined edge to his voice. "Now get outside and do your job."

"Acknowledged." Ra'Ewl ran from the living room.

Owens turned to look at Crissy; she was so very small, his armored gloves were massive by comparison. It would be so easy to unintentionally hurt her. "Sweetie, I need you to stand up, can you do that for me?" he said while nodding his head in the affirmative.

On shaky legs she stood. Owens helped to steady her, but in the back of his mind the fear that he might accidentally break her fought for his attention. Carefully he retrieved the blanket and placed it around her so that it could be pulled up over her head.

"Mommy!" Crissy cried in a hoarse voice; tears welling up in her eyes as she uselessly flung herself hard toward the body on the ground.

Owens held on to her, knowing too well that if she didn't calm down, this was not going to work. All he could think to do was fall back on what had comforted him. "Crissy, Sweetie, please look at me."

Her tear filled eye met his. "Sweetie, we have to go. Mommy is with God now, and I promise you, that after you have had a long and happy life, you'll be with her again." Owens' faith had always been strong, but in this day and age, God was often something other people talked about, not something they believed in.

It could have just been the look in Owens' eyes, or his sincere tone of voice, but Crissy stopped crying and fighting him. She closed her eyes and clung to him as if what he'd said had changed everything.

Relieved, Owens swung his weapon so that it rode under his right arm within easy reach of his hand. Snapping closed his visor he gently picked up the girl and carried her on his left arm, the thumb of that hand tucked into the webbing of his load-carrying gear. "Raul, Kizzy, status?"

"All clear," they replied.

"On the move."

The team moved through the darkness as if it held no domain over them. Once again they were operating on active night vision, as their infrared lamps punched small arcs of scenery out of the surrounding void. The Parrs were scouting ahead. Owens followed, trying to minimize bouncing the girl around as he negotiated the uneven, root-covered ground.

"Hold up!" instructed Ke'Se, excitement flavoring his words as he went to ground.

Ra'Ewl went down onto his stomach.

Turning off his helmet lamps, Ke'Se sat up. Ra'Ewl looked off into the same general direction to see what had attracted his comrade's attention. With his lights out, Ra'Ewl crept up on Ke'Se and then slowly sat up next to him. *"Where?"*

"At about thirty-degrees, something moved against the ambience of the clearing."

Through Ra'Ewl's scopes, the break in the trees shone like sunlight as seen at the far end of a dark tunnel. *"Suit, nine-power."* His display transitioned into a magnified view; now the slightest movement of his head was exaggerated. Looking down at his compass display, he aimed his head to thirty-degrees.

Intently, he scanned the area. There it was; a rounded, smooth shape, black against the background glow. It was moving to its left, toward another of its kind standing next to a tree. The silhouette was all too familiar.

"Owens, we have bad guys!" Ra'Ewl communed, not waiting for Owens to confirm he was listening.

"Raul, say again!"

"We have ECHOS between us and the recovery site!" repeated Ra'Ewl, making sure to emphasize the term Owens used for the bad guys.

Owens darted for cover behind a bank of surface roots. Like gigantic snakes they twisted around and over each other, covering the ground between the two massive trees. Bracing the girl with his free hand, Owens came to an abrupt halt behind the roots; going down onto one knee, he leaned forward so that only his head was above the edge.

Startled, Crissy cried out.

In the still air of the forest, the sound carried; bouncing off into the distance.

The Parrs turned in response; Owens icon was at the epicenter.

Ra'Ewl swung back to reacquire the bad guys, things had changed. "Owens, the Echoes are on the move."

"Roger that," replied Owens. He turned to the little girl.

"Sweetie, please quiet down," he pleaded, his helmet just inches away from her. No good. "Kizzy, get back here. Raul, maintain contact, and make damn sure you don't get between us and the Echoes," he ordered.

Pulling the blanket up around her head, Owens carefully placed the girl down into a gap among the roots. "Crissy, you need to stay here," he told her. She was already trying to work her way free. Owens used careful force to keep her in place.

Ke'Se landed with a soft thump, his IR lamps on low barely lit up the scene; Owens was always astonished at just how fast a Parr could run. "Suit, external, disengage." He was now back on comm traffic only. "You keep her here anyway you can." He gestured for Ke'Se to take over. "Knock her down and sit on her if you have to, just keep her under cover."

The Parr moved around Owens' legs, and up under his arms; with outstretched paws he took over. "How do I keep her quiet?"

Owens moved back and reached for his weapon. With one smooth motion he brought his square-framed rifle up and placed it at the ready. On his visor's display the weapon's semicircular targeting reticle appeared, its PIP (Projected Impact Point) dot resting at its center. "You don't." He then moved off.

"Ra'Ewl, what do we have?" Owens was moving quickly to gain distance from the girl.

"Two, possibly three Echoes, moving toward your..." Ra'Ewl looked back, Owens' icon was moving up off to his right. He corrected his response, "Ke'Se's position. They're just over a hundred yards ahead of me."

"Stay left and close to fifty. Then bunker down."

"Acknowledged." Ra'Ewl sped off.

Owens was still covering ground, all the time looking for an advantageous place to set up his ambush. "On station," came over the comm from

Ra'Ewl. *The time is now*, Owens thought. Just ahead was another ancient tree. Its trunk was easily six yards across, with massive surface roots splayed out from its buttress.

He moved into position behind the tree. Looking around, he tried to memorize the position of the potentially foot-tripping roots. With his left hand against the tree, he turned off his IR lamps and maneuvered around the trunk.

Now in relative darkness, he could see the distant glow from the far-off clearing; Ra'Ewl's green icon shown off to his left. Intently, he scanned the arc between himself, the Parr, and the clearing. His eyes locked onto two sets of small lights. A sudden feeling of intense anticipation washed over him, not unlike a child forced to wait to open a present.

Bracing himself against the tree, he raised his weapon. With a squeeze of his right hand, he depressed the leading edge of the rifle's handgrip; *Click*. The safeties were off and power made available. A pull of the two-fingered trigger would now launch a salvo of electromagnetically accelerated, armor-piercing darts.

Owens settled his sight's PIP onto the further of the two. "Firing!" he warned his comrades over the comm, as his darts cracked through the air, breaking the sound barrier. The first target bounced from the hits, but without waiting for it to drop he swung onto the second. He couldn't hear the concluding thump of his projectiles as they punched through mesh body armor to render flesh and smash bone, but he knew with satisfaction they had hit.

He released the trigger and the world went quiet, nothing moved. Owens took in a breath; he had been holding it while he fired. Although it had only been a few seconds, his body demanded air.

"On the move," called Owens as he stepped forward over the root. He'd heard the *thump* and caught sight of the flash; in that moment, his training took over as muscle memory tried to drive him to safety.

Everything was a blur of motion as the world flew past at strange angles; memories of being in the heart of a blazing fire raced in his mind. He could hear breathing, it was becoming louder and labored, his eyes snapped open; it was him.

"Status," he choked. Coughing, he spat up something; it had a strong metallic taste.

"Corporal Owens, you are critically injured," stated the Pacscomp in its emotionally neutral female voice.

Owens fought to reorient himself; he was prone and lying on his left side. As he kicked out with his right leg, a wave of pain slashed through him. The momentum rolled him onto his back, the pain forcing his eyes shut, trapping him in hell. "Combat!" he screamed past the pain.

"Corporal Owens, the administering of Comburodorphin in your current state could result in exsanguination," it said calmly.

"Do it!" he demanded. The threat of bleeding out from the Combat drug seemed meaningless.

The initial sensation of the transdermal spray hitting the base of Owens' neck was lost to him. Then the drug reached his brain, and the pain faded away. It felt like cool water was running through his vein, as the drugs' synthetic hormones and endorphins dominated his body. His eyes dilated in response, and his mind finally cleared.

"*Ne se deplacent pas!*" someone yelled in French.

Owens could feel his heart pounding in his chest, as his reality shifted into slow motion. He looked up; standing there just on the other side of the surface root was a Legionnaire. A bullpup assault rifle pointed at Owens, the mercenary's hand gripping the weapon's underslung 30mm grenade launcher.

"Don't move!" the gunman restated in English.

Something was moving fast at the edge of Owens' display. Like some mystical creature of the forest, it seemed to fly through the air toward the enemy. It was Ra'Ewl's icon. With a *thud*, the scout connected high on the mercenary's back, knocking him forward over the root, toward Owens.

Startled, the mercenary pushed out his left arm in an effort to break his fall; the assault rifle still held by its pistol grip in the other.

Owen reared up to meet him; making a desperate grab for control of his opponent's weapon, he did manage to shove it aside as the gunman landed on top of him. Now as the tide of battle shifted, Owens wrapped his left arm around the mercenary's neck and grabbed for the back of his equipment harness, pinning his face down onto Owens' chest.

Panicking, the mercenary fought to bring his legs up under him in the hopes of pushing free.

Owens held tight as he threw his own leg across the captive's. He then grabbed for his knife, and with a *snap*, pulled it free from its sheath. With a hard thrust, the thick blade's reinforced chiseled tip punched through the mercenary's mesh armor, and sank deep into the side of his throat; his whole body jerked as the edge struck home.

Like a vise, the mercenary locked his hand onto Owens' knife-wielding arm; desperately he pulled at his tormentor. Owens knew it was just a matter of time; he could feel his captive's strength failing, as fingers lost their hold and went limp. With a twist, he pulled the knife free to an accompanying gush of arterial spray. A sensation of warmth was conveyed across his gloves' tactile contact pads; blood continued to pump from the opening.

"Tae the Devil with ya!" yelled Owens as he pushed the still twitching body of the mercenary aside; it rolled over and landed with a *thump* onto its back, bending its right arm at an unnatural angle and trapping the assault rifle underneath.

Owens turned to look for his own weapon; it lay just a few feet away tethered to him by its strap. Planting his knife in the ground, he reached out, his fingers closed around its roll-bar hand guard. He pulled the rifle into his arms and made it ready.

"Owens?" said a familiar voice. Standing on the chest of the fallen mercenary was Ra'Ewl, his head darting about as he attempted to take stock of the situation.

Owens took a deep breath, something wasn't right. "Yeah, I'm with you."

Ra'Ewl lowered himself down onto his belly, seemingly to get a better look. "Your left thigh is a mess. Can you walk?"

Owens knew the answer. He placed his gauss rifle on the ground, and then patted his chest. "Come here."

Ra'Ewl paused for just a moment, then stood up, walked over, and settled down onto Owens, who was now reaching into his side pack. Owens placed his hand on the Parr's backpack, where he then flipped up a small metal loop and held it in place. In his other hand was the connector end for the emergency carry strap, which if need be, he could use to sling a Parr like a piece of equipment; it *snapped* as he hooked it in to the ring.

"Get her to the recovery site."

Ra'Ewl stood up and climbed carefully up toward Owens face. There he stood for just a moment, as if he could see in through the helmet's frontal armor. "*Roger*," he replied, then turned and headed off.

Owens sat with his back against the tree, his gauss rifle across his lap. The damage to his thigh was horrendous, but he did what he could. He'd used up the medpack's coagulant spray in an effort to slow down the blood loss and now only a pressure bandage kept him from bleeding out. Tingles ran down his neck as the suit administered drugs to help keep him stable.

"We'll be on the ground in less than fifteen," stated an unseen voice. "Just hang in there."

"Roger that." Owens closed his eyes; the suit had lowered its internal temperature to an uncomfortable level in order buy its user a little more time. He could feel his hot breath blowing past his cheeks. There was a glow beyond his eyelids, something was flickering.

He struggled to open his eyes as he turned his head; arm muscles twitched in an effort to raise his weapon from his lap, but to no avail. About ten yards away was a moving pool of white light; through his scopes it blazed like a searchlight. Owens smiled. Ra'Ewl had turned on his helmet lamps, and with Crissy in tow holding tight onto his carry handle, he was guiding her through the darkness. She stamped along behind him in her oversized boots, while holding her blue plushy rabbit high up under her left arm.

"I know how you feel," joked Owens, remembering the contact bandage that Ra'Ewl had put across the rabbit's soft belly.

Ke'Se was just behind them; he stopped and looked in Owens direction. An unspoken sense of kinship seemed to pass between them. Owens raised his hand and motioned for Ke'Se to keep moving. At a trot Ke'Se caught up with the others.

Once they had gone, he was alone in the dark; the sounds of comm traffic from the approaching ADF tilt-rotor aircraft played in the background. His mind started to wander; it had found its way back to Crissy's house, and the sight of her eyes wide with terror. Owens looked over at the dead Legionnaire, then thought about the other two he'd taken out, and nodded with satisfaction. "Now there are three less wolves."

Everyone needs to prove themselves. Both to themselves and to the people around them, some more than others. It is said that no plan survives its execution on the battlefield and sometimes those plans go horribly wrong. And others produce unexpected results.

Greg Schauer

PROVING OUT

Danielle Ackley-McPhail

THE MISSION WASN'T ANYWHERE NEAR SANCTIONED. BUT IT WAS TRADITION.

For the decades there had been an air base on the planet Demeter, newbies had shed their down feathers on just such shenanigans as this. It was a challenge to keep it fresh and new, bordering just on the correct side of reckless. The current batch of pilots—one of whom had grown up on bedtime stories of her older brother's fledgling run—had shown up to roll call yesterday and proposed their own proving out. With a gleam in her eye, Captain Jayne "Scarlet Jay" Corvidae gave them the nod, pleased with their initiative.

Now she stared down another dawn waiting for her chicks to come home.

"You do realize they didn't tell you everything, yeah?" First Lieutenant Chen "Raven" Po murmured, her face serene, as always, though her dark brown eyes had clouded near to black.

Jay remained silent a moment as she turned to scan the sky, her eyes tracking the dissipating contrails. "Yeah, I'd say that's a given," she answered, still scanning. A slight frown slid over her lips and she narrowed her gaze. Something was off here. There were only three trails...and they didn't match those left by the unit's assigned craft. She didn't think too hard on why. That was what the proving out was about, new pilots showing they were capable of independent thought and strategic planning. Not to mention a bit of crazy-ass madness thrown in. Per tradition, she and Raven had diplomatically not been there for the takeoff. Now curiosity ate an ever-growing hole in her focus. *What the hell else were they up to?*

The sound of the airfield personnel coming off shift interrupted her thoughts. Slowly Jay and Raven turned and headed for the barracks lest someone notice the attention they paid to the star-studded sky. Plausible deniability only got you so far.

The fledgling flight wing came in along the Allied side of the demilitarized zone, well into their own territory and away from the demarcation line, the pilots keeping the jets below the cirrus deck. Kyle "Flash" Panski readied his gear for possible evac. His nerves danced as he eyeballed the inky black beyond the jet's canopy, head rolling back as he strained to see any sign they had company, beyond the two jets flanking them. He reached a hand up to brace his helmet as the weight of the infra-red goggles perched on top pulled everything back against the strap securing it under his chin.

Flash chaffed at not being at the controls. They flew tandem for this mission in borrowed jets, rather than their usual, single-seat PlasmaHawks. His wingman, Thom "Bang" Masson, won the draw for the pilot seat. Pulling this mission off required they fly in two-man teams: one to drop for ground reconnaissance, if needed, and one to circle. The only jets at the base with that capacity were the Harbingers. Each pilot in their flight had bartered away a few hours of extra duty to get the airmen assigned the craft they now flew to look the other way. Technically, there were regulations against stationed crew "swapping" hours—not to mention aircraft—but the corps was big on supporting tradition. During proving-out missions the higher ups overlooked a lot.

A slight frown on his face, Flash turned his gaze to the dual monitor set into the console in front of him. One side showed a reference video of the terrain below as of last night's patrol. The other displayed a real-time video feed of the same landscape. Both were night-vision enhanced. Though the monitoring system would alert him to any variation, Flash scanned for anomalies anyway. Six weeks ago he had taken his first flight over these grounds. It started as a simple patrol, but he and Captain Corvidae ended up in an unexpected dogfight. Their only warning had been an alert from the video scan.

Thanks to his malfunctioning NovaStream jet, Flash did more dodging than fighting in that first encounter. But Scarlet Jay? She handed the Dominion their asses. Ground patrols were still coming across bits of wreckage from the Hyperwing drones and Boru fighters downed in that encounter.

Things had been quiet since then, but the Dominion forces weren't known for sitting back and just taking a rocket to the teeth like they'd gotten from Captain Corvidae. Call it cliché, but everyone knew they were up to something. Time to find out what...

But not all in a snarl like this. Flash had to get his focus back. A couple of deep breaths loosened his taut muscles—all but his gut—and he brought his mind back to the mission. According to reports, there were signs of activity across the DMZ. Recent patrols had flagged a few zones close to Allied territory for anomalies. Command had deemed the risk level low. They'd increased patrols, but would not authorize squad deployment into the demilitarized zone to confirm and neutralize the threat. Flash grimaced. He'd seen the reports, recognized similarities in the images. He also knew firsthand how ruthless the Dominion could be. From a military standpoint, the order to disregard the anomalies made no sense. Unless... If Flash had to guess, someone was coming up for reelection had made it clear to military command that they didn't want the current conflict to escalate until after they'd won their race.

Whatever the reason, it sat wrong with the 66th's annex wing. As service men and women they had all taken oaths to stand against any threats, foreign, domestic, or interstellar. Based on that intel, Flash and his wing mates were out here on their own time and under the radar to find and disable any new sensors the Dominion may have planted on or near Allied soil. The original sensors that had led to Flash's first combat had been neutralized by the crews on ground patrol, but any possibility there were more out there needed to be confirmed and dealt with. The plan was to fly a grid pattern over the zones in question. If the monitoring system sent up any flags the jets would land and drop members of the wing for a manual inspection while the Harbingers returned to the air, scanning for aerial threats. If there was nothing there, fine, but if there was...all they had to do was find one sensor and Command would have a reason to take official action. If necessary, the wing would extend their inspection out in a radial pattern from the initial anomaly point until they were certain the zones were clean.

Good thing the nights are long on Demeter this time of year. With a sigh lamenting the loss of sleep, Flash glanced over at his wingman. To be heard over the engines, he spoke into the mic along the edge of his comm hood. "ETA?"

"T-minus fifteen minutes," Bang answered as he manipulated the controls in preparation for a gradual descent.

Flash's shoulders twitched. They were about to come down to it. The proving out. Six weeks and a world of change had gone by and after tonight everyone who mattered would see whether or not he—and the others in his wing—had what it took to serve in the air corps. There was no overcoming those nerves. He didn't have any doubts about the others; they were crack pilots and soldiers. But him? There were years of inexcusable arrogance and entitlement to purge, not to mention self-serving habits to break. There were disadvantages growing up the son of a president. Even he had to admit that when he'd got here he'd been an insufferable prick. Had he truly transformed as much as he wanted to believe he had?

Something of his mood must have broadcasted through the cabin because beside him Bang reached out with his right hand and knuckled Flash's helmet. "Shake it off, man. It's almost time to play."

Flash blew out another long breath, cracked his neck from side to side, and ran a system check on the guns to make sure his gear was in order. As the airman in the second seat, he stood in as gunner. Satisfied, he leaned forward and focused his full attention on the dual monitor as they neared one of the flagged zones. They didn't expect trouble. The mission should be a cake-run; fly in, scan, and get the hell back to base before anyone in command had time to complain.

He hoped things were as simple as that. The Harbingers ran light on rockets and heavy on guns. Not the best combination if they actually had to engage the enemy. Given the advancements in armored aircraft being flown, unless a pilot or gunner got real lucky, it took too long to gun something out of the sky. During standard aerial combat, Harbingers were used in conjunction with more heavily armed craft because of their maneuverability. While they dove in to harass, the PlasmaHawks and NovaStreams came in for the kill. On their own, the Harbingers just didn't have the weight to go up against a wing of Boru 47-V's or more than a couple of Hyperwing drones. That should be a non-issue, though.

"Okay, time to get to work, slacker," Bang said as he toggled a switch and brought up the Harbinger's transparent, head's-up display. A small green dot showed the Harbinger on the edge of the grid. Flash brought his hands to his console, keying in commands to engage the exterior antenna that scanned for the type of electronic signatures typical of the kind of flight sensors they were searching for. He then locked his eyes on the dual monitors in front of him as they began their methodical fly-over.

Up and back they bisected the zone.

The roar of the engines intensified as Bang brought them down in a vertical landing maneuver reminiscent of the old Harrier jets the Harbingers were patterned on. With barely a bump, the wheels met the deck. Flash released his safety harness and popped his side of the canopy. Pivoting as his feet hit the ground, he crouched and moved several meters off where he watched Bang close the canopy and lift off once more. The jet ran dark, the pilots depending on the internal sensors to coordinate their relative positions. By the time the Harbinger climbed twenty feet up into the night sky Flash had lost sight of the craft. He turned and gave his eyes a moment to acclimate to the darkness. Every muscle tensed. Already he missed the subtle vibration of the jet's engines and the lingering scent of rocket fuel. Basic training aside ground-pounding was not a natural state for a pilot. Regardless, an airman needed to be versatile, capable of responding to unexpected combat situations outside of their field of expertise. Flash had every intention of rising to the occasion, even if it meant keeping his feet on the ground.

Slowly he trailed his gaze over the nearby terrain, getting a feel for his surroundings before he engaged his IR goggles and turned on the camouflage circuit built into his gear. The wildlife had gone into silent mode, the only sound the rustle of the breeze through the light brush blanketing the ground. A faint ping from his earphone signaled an incoming hail.

"Airmen, report." The voice belonged to Keeli "Hawk" Hawkins. Her skill at the stick made her the ranking pilot among their wing and thus in charge of the mission. That would have rankled six weeks ago, but Flash respected and trusted his wing mates, Hawk in particular, in a way he hadn't been capable of when he'd arrived.

Flexing his jaw, he activated his mic and drew his goggles into place. "Flash reporting, wheels on the ground and ready." Keying in the command on his field data unit, he transmitted his coordinates to his wing mates. In an orderly manner, the others called in their confirmations. Flash's data unit beeped in rapid succession as he received their coordinates in return.

"Okay, move 'em out," Hawk said. "Check-in is every sixty. You find anything, do not move it. Flag it and call it in. We do not know what kind of defenses the Demons might have added to the package after they lost their last batch of sensors. Acknowledged?"

Like a mass echo, everyone responded, "Acknowledged."

The night grew old. In the far distance to his left the faintest edge of grey limned the horizon. Two check-ins had gone by with nothing much to show for the time. Flash was reminded of the old military adage: long hours of intense boredom punctuated by brief moments of sheer terror. Pushing that thought aside, he continued his methodical sweep of the zone, eyes trained on his data unit, which also served as a portable scanner programmed to identify military hardware. So far, all it had turned up were more wreckage fragments. As he drew closer to the DMZ, Flash began to wonder if they'd come out on a snipe hunt.

A ping sounded from his earphone. Flash activated his mic. "Go."

"Hawk here, be alert. Bulldog reports signs of activity in his zone, a break in the ground cover and a disturbed patch of dirt about the size of a Dominion sensor."

"Acknowledged," Flash responded, as he stooped to create a lower profile. He moved with more care as he continued to scan the landscape. When he reached the service road that marked the Allied border he hunkered down, not quite covered by the low brush, but blending with it as the camouflage circuit altered the pattern on his gear. He kept his face angled down and did a slow inspection of the surrounding terrain. The local equivalent of a wildcat padded by about ten meters out, some small creature dangling from its mouth, but all else was quiet. No movement, no sounds, and yet an air of tension blanketed what remained of the night. Flash stay where he crouched until the scheduled patrol went by. He gave them ten minutes to get clear, then crossed the service road into the DMZ still in a crouch, rapidly moving away out of sight.

As he pressed deeper into no man's land, there was a *whir* right by his head and something cracked the air like a sail snapping with the wind. Flash ducked and brought his rifle up. The sound repeated and he cursed under his breath, feeling ridiculous. Somewhere too nearby, hidden by a cluster of brush, was a ground owl nest. The *whir* was mama owl dive-bombing him to warn him off. Relaxing his grip the slightest bit, Flash lowered the barrel of his rifle to standby.

A faint pulse on his arm alerted him that the data unit had identified something. He glanced down and corrected his position to head for the coordinates. Flash moved forward, sliding his feet carefully to avoid stepping into Mama's nest. A rustle in the ground cover followed his movement. There was another *whir*. This one sounded a bit fainter...further off. Behind him. Flash spun and brought his weapon to bear, tracking over the barrel. Before he could lock on a target something solid...much bigger than a ground owl...connected with his back, slamming him forward into the ground. At the same time an arm reached out and snatched away his rifle.

Flash tried to roll away, but something...some*one*, pinned his shoulders down and shoved their knee into his back. He bucked against their grip but did not have the leverage to break free. There was not much call for hand-to-hand in the cockpit of a plane and Flash had been regrettably lax in practicing what he'd learned in Basic. He froze at a movement coming toward them.

Out of the dark the silhouette of a man took shape. If Flash remembered his Dominion markings right, this one was a sergeant. As the soldier passed a particularly large clump of dying brush he reached out and grabbed it. A tug pulled it from the ground, revealing a sensor hidden beneath. Dropping the bush, he continued stalking forward, stopping just out of reach of Flash's hands. Not that coming closer would have mattered. The monkey on Flash's back had him pinned in such a way that he could not feel his arms, let alone move them.

The sergeant mocked him with a *tsk* before he accepted Flash's rifle from his partner. Releasing the clip, the man pocketed the ammunition and tossed the weapon out into the dark. With a sneer he looked down at Flash.

"The Alliance, they are sending out little boys to do the work of men now?" he said with traces of a Slavic accent before he turned away, his head shaking.

Baring his teeth, Flash growled and tried to hump up his back to dislodge his attacker. The soldier who had turned away spun and lashed out, his boot connecting hard with the side of Flash's head. His helmet absorbed part of the impact, but his vision still swam and a roaring sound filled his ears. Over the roar he could just barely hear his first attacker laugh. Flash forced his thoughts to focus. Lowering his head with an artful groan, he flexed his jaw to activate his mic. A faint *ping* in his earpiece told him he'd connected. He spoke before anyone on the other end could.

"That's a nice sensor you have there...didn't know they grew wild..." The words came out slurred, but that didn't dull their impact. The Dominion soldier spun around again and looked ready to let loose with another kick. Why he resisted, Flash couldn't say but the man's eyes narrowed as he dropped down and moved in close. He reached out and released the strap holding Flash's helmet, then shoved it back off of his face. The Dominion soldier activated a helmet-mounted light. Flash squeezed his eyes shut against the brightness and tried to duck his head, but a hand grabbed his chin and forced his head back. Then the hand jerked away and a stream of curses peppered the night.

"You remember this, president's son....we didn't set these and we will not sit back while the Alliance creates an incident and blames it on us, hear?"

Flash blinked and tried to focus, but the man before him blurred. "Whatever you say, boss. That is not a Dominion sensor and I am not being restrained by Dominion soldiers. Got it."

The soldier growled and spat in the dirt by Flash's face, before rising to walk back toward the sensor.

"Let him go," the man called over his shoulder as he quickly knelt and extracted the sensor, sliding it into a frame pack he then secured and slid onto his shoulders. The one holding Flash tightened his grip and argued back in rapid-fire Russian.

"*Now!*" the first soldier ordered. "I will not be the one to hand the Alliance a weapon against us. He is one, ill-trained boy. Kill him and he is a rallying point against us. Let him live, and he is a message. Now hurry up, before his friends arrive."

The pressure lifted from Flash's back. He tried to rear up, but what felt like a rifle stock connected with the back of his head. As he slumped down to the ground the Demons disappeared into the twilight as the sound of Harbinger jets filled the sky.

Crest of The Ty'Pherrien Alliance,
Allied Defence Force

As DC comics used to call them, this is an imaginary story using characters from the Alliance Archives universe. Originally written for the collection Stories in Between, it takes place in a very different world from the one these soldiers are used to fighting in.

Greg Schauer

BEYOND IMAGINE

Mike McPhail

"As soldiers, we may all fight together, but we die alone."
—William Kriegherren

THERE WAS THE SOUND OF BREATHING—VERY CLOSE AND CONFINED. INGRAM SENSED the rise and fall of his chest, and realized that it was in unison with the sounds. Hot air flowed back against his face with each breath. It was as if he was just an observer in all this; there, but not a part of it.

Muffled voices filtered in to the enclosed space. He couldn't understand them, but subconsciously they represented a comfortable connection. The world around him was black, still, and without meaningful form. Then something shifted nearby. He could feel it. His eyes snapped open and consciousness rushed over him; he was back. *But back from where?* he thought.

His body suddenly spasmed, trying to move in any way it could, but to no avail. He was trapped.

Panic welled up from the hardwired part of his brain; hormones surged and his breathing quickened.

There's no air. He wanted to scream.

If you panic, you're as good as dead, yelled a voice in his head.

"Stonebridge," he panted, finding reassurance in the memory of his combat instructor; a man who could have been punched from the same mold as every British drill instructor throughout history.

Assess your situation, the voice said, *and then work with what you've got. Don't panic, Death will just have to wait its turn.*

Calmer now, Ingram slowed his breathing and tried to concentrate. He still couldn't move. "Hello," he called. His voice sounded muffled to his ears, like he was... "Damnit," he said, cursing his own stupidity.

"Suit-mode, power up." In a flurry of lights and sounds—and an accompanying rush of cool air—his helmet displays came to life; the world outside remained black, except for the familiar green triangular identification icons; one topped with MGN floated just before him.

His comm crackled, and her voice sounded by his ear. "Ingram, can you hear me?"

"Yeah, I'm with you, Morgan."

"Stay calm and engage your active light-amp; we'll have you out of there in just a moment."

"Acknowledged," he said. "Suit-mode, active night-vision." The suit's on-board computer—Pacscomp—turned the scene into a daytime-bright, false-color image, lit by a cluster of infrared diodes mounted on either side of his helmet. Although distorted and washed out due to bounce back from some sort of transparent covering, he could easily make out the smooth, body-armor carapace of his fellow troopers. To an outsider, they could have easily been mistaken for faceless creatures of war; they would have been half right. These were soldiers of the Allied Defense Force, his comrades in arms; more importantly, they were his friends.

Morgan stared straight back at him and waved while the other trooper— his icon read MKC—seemed preoccupied with something just off to the right.

"Morgan, what's going on?" Ingram asked.

"Got it, give me a hand." MacKencey, the other trooper, called to Morgan as he secured his fighting knife. Together they pulled aside the thick transparency entombing him, but Ingram still couldn't move.

"Almost done," Morgan said as she put her hand firmly on his chest, holding him still.

There was a snipping sound, and suddenly he could move his legs, then his arms. He reached up and grabbed Morgan's forearm.

"Easy, sir," MacKencey said as he came into view, now holding a pair of wire cutters. With his other hand, he tipped Ingram's head back, and moved in toward his throat.

Snip. Ingram immediately found himself slumping forward. If not for Morgan's hand bracing him, he would have fallen. He felt like he still might. He tried to shift his weight to compensate, but it was no good; he was too stiff and had a hard time just moving.

"We have you," Morgan said as she and MacKencey helped him shift position.

Ingram grabbed hold of MacKencey's shoulder and worked himself loose. "Thanks."

MacKencey tapped him on the shoulder in response, and then stepped around him. Morgan moved back and un-slung her gauss rifle.

Ingram stood there for a moment and took in the scene; they were in an enclosed compound, a massive storage area of some kind. He couldn't see much detail across the distance, and no color through the night-amp setting, but the place reminded him of the supply depot on base, only on a gigantic scale. He couldn't even hazard a guess at the items he was seeing, but if it was anything like Supply, there was everything imaginable between these walls. The architecture itself was comprised of many flat surfaces which met at 90-degree angles to form what appeared to be free standing buildings inside of the main structure extending well beyond the edge of his scope's range. All of those he could see were crammed full of whatever this place supplied. The ground level was covered in some type of composite or laminate; it was dirty white, with a slight sheen to the surface.

Off in the distance, two more troopers slowly moved about—icons BUR and KTV—while icon MRU floated near the bottom of his screen. A Parr scout sat upright just a few feet away, his head slightly cocked to one side as he contemplated Ingram in that all too familiar way that only a cat can. Ingram resisted the urge to bend down and pet him. Kind of senseless as the cat, too, was clad in lightweight-polymer armor. But nevertheless, the sight of the Parr and his fellow troopers was comforting.

"Okay, Morgan, fill me in." It was more of a command than a request.

Morgan paused for a moment before answering. "I woke up over there, laying on the ground out in the open." She pointed toward the remains of a container; its transparent facing had been torn off. "Beyond that, I'm a blank. Not sure how I got free."

MacKencey reappeared holding a gauss rifle and several magazines. "Here you go, sir."

With a nod, Ingram took the ammo and secured it to his carrying gear, then ran a quick check on the weapon.

"There was no one in sight," Morgan said. "Then I saw the other capsules all lined up." She gestured behind Ingram, who turned in response. The container he had just been liberated from stood at the end of the line between two parallel rails. There were markings on every surface, interspersed with graphic images, his face disturbingly among them, but he couldn't decipher the meaning of it all. It was still secure between opposing sets of notches; there were spaces for five other containers. "Mac was in the second capsule..."

"Sarcophagus might be a better description," MacKencey said. "After all, they did pack us off in full armor, with hardware."

Ingram held up his hand. "Please continue, corporal."

She shifted her weight from one leg to the other, as if the thought made her uneasy. "I could see there was an ADF trooper inside, but there was no Pacscomp activity." She looked away for a moment. "Nor any bio-signs; no movement, venting, or even residual heat. I though he was dead." she looked over at MacKencey.

"Sorry, maybe next time," he said.

Ingram slung his weapon across his chest, and then made a quick head-count. Six slots, six troopers present, and six containers lay open. "Is there anyone else?"

"No, sir, you're the last one we know of," Morgan said. "Also there's no comm traffic beyond the squad-ban. Sergeant Bauer has a signal booster, but that's also a negative. Sir, we're not even picking up the local Comm or Navsats."

"Right." Ingram ran through the possible ramifications.

"Ah, sir..." MacKencey said, almost apologetically.

Ingram paused for a moment before answering. "Yes?"

MacKencey took a deep breath before continuing. "What's the last thing you remember?" he asked. It almost sounded as if he already knew the answer.

"I..." Ingram drew a blank. "I've got nothing."

"Do you remember home?" Morgan asked.

Ingram just stood there, a sense of despair pushing at him deep and hard. He looked over at Morgan and just shook his head.

"But you do remember us?" she asked.

"Yes, that much is clear," he said with a feeling of some certainty against the unknown. Anything related to his military career was solidly in place, like it was hardwired. Everything else.... *Damnit*, he thought, *you're the one in charge, so be in charge, take control of the situation, not the other way around.*

"Right, everyone form up," he said over the squad-band.

"Acknowledged," voices chorused from his comhood's speakers, as the other troopers jogged over to join them.

Now together, Ingram took stock. Everyone was outfitted with what the ADF called AS-Is (Allied Standard-Issue) as far as individual weapons, ammunition loads, and munitions. The heaviest weapon belonged to Sergeant Kotov, the team's gunner: the medium gauss rifle—the ADF's base-of-fire machinegun. The massive piece of hardware was typically hung from a shoulder sling and rested at the user's hip. The sergeant, not being typical, used it like a rifle.

Your men are counting on you to have the answers, Stonebridge said from the recesses of Ingram's mind. *Never be indecisive; make a decision, even if you have no way of knowing whether it's right or wrong. YOU have to make a decision.*

"Listen up..." Ingram said, forced to rely on his common sense until something better came along. "We need to check the area for anyone else. Have any of you had a chance to look around?"

"Da, Centurion," Kotov said, pointing off into the darkness. His other hand rested gently against the side of his weapon to keep it from swinging, as it now hung loosely from its straps. "At about twelve meters there is a sheer drop-off that runs in both directions out beyond my scopes."

"We also have a bit of high ground back that way," Bauer said, gesturing behind the group. "Like everything else so far, it seems to be made up of multilevel platforms packed with storage containers of some sort; it goes well up over twenty meters higher than any point in this place."

Ingram turned; he could just make out the structure.

"This place reminds me of the cargo staging area at Churchill Spaceport," MacKencey said. "You know, that place where they off-load the box containers from the trains, then stack them up for later use?"

"So are you saying someone packed us off for shipment?" Bauer tightened his grip on his weapon.

"I don't know. I'm just saying this looks like a storage hanger." MacKencey said.

"Are we inside a building?" Morgan asked.

"Most likely," Kotov said. "Look up, no stars, not even overcast glow."

MacKencey stared up. "If we are inside, then this space must be at least as big as a Terran sports stadium."

Stay on top of things, Squad Leader.

"Okay, just put that on the growing list of things we need to find out. Until we do I want everyone to maintain light-discipline; I.R. only." Ingram waited a moment. "Understood?"

"Acknowledged," the team replied.

"Sergeant," Ingram said, looking at Bauer. "Deploy a beacon; we'll use this as our rally point."

Bauer pulled what looked like a small, rounded can from his side pouch. Unscrewing the top, he depressed the activation button. Throughout the team, a yellow icon appeared on their displays, bearing the label RP01. The sergeant then placed the can down among the remains of a container.

"Good. Has anyone scouted beyond this point?" Ingram asked, gesturing toward a wall of boxes opposite of the drop off. The reply was "negative."

"All right then; MacKencey, you and Ma'Rou do what you do best." He motioned them off in that direction, then turned back to the others. "Morgan, you head for that high ground Bauer scoped out; we could do with a little bird's eye view of this place."

"Sergeants," he said, pointing at Bauer and Kotov. "Check out the other side of that wall, while I go with Morgan. Any questions?" There were none. "Move out."

"I still think it's some type of test," Ma'Rou psicommed over the team-band; he was currently riding on top of MacKencey's pack, facing back.

Nature hadn't equipped the Parr with the ability to speak any known human language, and in fact they didn't even try. Instituted in the early testing phase of Doctor McPherren's Synaptic Interface, a system that allowed direct mind-machine communication, the Parr's thoughts were interpreted and synthesized into speech by the suit's Pacscomp.

MacKencey only half-listened, his weapon at the ready as he moved across the maze-like terrain. "So, Mr. Sterling, who do you think managed to pull this off?" he asked, as he approached a tall, narrow gap in the structure.

"My first guess would be the Ka'nigits," Ma'Rou said.

"The Ka'nigits?" MacKencey laughed. "Right. You've been hanging out with our expatriate friends again."

Ma'Rou's tail twitched with uncertainty. *"Yeah, they let us watch those old movies."*

Mackencey smiled at the thought of a dozen sentient house cats sitting around a theater display, trying to interpret what humans thought was funny almost a century ago. "The colonel is the only person in the known universe who refers to the Teutonic Knights as Ka'nigits. True, they're an elitist, techno-terrorist group, with more money than common sense, but that's still no reason to be rude."

"Is that a bad thing?" Ma'Rou asked, as he nervously started kneading the pack.

MacKencey stopped and peered around the edge of the gap; it was black beyond the opening. Looking up, he judged the height to the top of the next platform.

"Can you make that jump?" he asked.

Ma'Rou sat up on the pack without answering. MacKencey felt the Parr revving up for the leap; he barely had time to brace before the fifteen pounds of armored cat pushed off his pack like a spring. Ma'Rou caught the edge of the landing with his back legs—his armor's claws dug into the side—he then pushed off to land with a thump somewhere on top.

"Okay, give me an—"

Ma'Rou's scream of terror flooded the comm.

It was like climbing on some over-sized child's playground. The box containers came in several sizes, and many could easily be stacked to act as steps. Morgan had just climbed up onto one of the bigger boxes when she suddenly doubled over as if to instinctively protect herself from some unseen horror. The impulse was external and not unfamiliar. Not even her superiors were aware, but she sensed things that were emotionally charged. She turned and looked off in the direction her squad mates had gone. Something was wrong.

"Morgan?" Ingram said.

"Sir..." She pointed off into the distance, just as MacKencey's voice came over the comm.

"—under attack! Ma'Rou's mis—" the message ended in a burst of static.

Ingram turned, looking for his trooper's icon. MRU was nowhere to be seen, while the MKC switched from the familiar green to a bright red with a time stamp, recording the moment the suit's Pacscomp self-destructed upon the perceived death of its user.

"MacKencey!" Bauer yelled over the comm. "Mac! Damnit, trooper, what is your status?"

Ingram forced his voice to remain calm. "MacKencey, Ma'Rou, report." Despite what the technology said, there was always a chance.

"It's no good, sir," Morgan said, her voice now steeled against the reality; she then turned and continued her climb. "Nothing can sneak up on me here, sir, I recommend that you join up with the others."

Ingram thought it over as he watched the two sergeants' icons heading for MacKencey's death marker; "Acknowledged, Corporal, keep me informed," he said as he slung his weapon and started down.

The troopers' jog slowed to a walk as they approached their target, cautiously moving beyond the stack of massive storage boxes. Kotov carried his weapon at the hip, moving it slowly from side to side to keep its momentum up; on his display, its targeting reticle and pip floated ethereally out in front of him. Bauer flanked him to his left; his own weapon was up and at the ready. They stopped. Bauer turned so he was standing almost back to back with Kotov.

The death marker was somewhere on the other side of a low wall of a stone-like substance jutting out across their path. To their left was a massive, one-story structure extended off into the distance, it appeared to be a glass-enclosed holding area. On their right was the drop off.

"I'm moving up to the wall," Kotov said, already on the move.

"Acknowledged." Bauer swung around, and aimed past his comrade.

Kotov stood facing the wall. "Suit-mode, gun view." An inset screen opened at the bottom of his display, showing a live feed from the targeting scopes mounted on the nose of his weapon. He slowly moved it out, and away from cover.

The image was surreal; Kotov wasn't a religious man *per se*, but he was brought up within the teachings of the Church. At this moment, he truly did believe in the existence of hell. After all, that's where demons came from.

At first it was hard to make out what was going on without a point of reference. Then Kotov spotted what he assumed was Mac's body face down on the ground, his standard-issue back pack clearly visible. In comparison the man-like beings were short and compact, only about four feet tall. They were clad in some type of sloped body-armor, made up of rows of smaller overlapping plates.

Three of the things were searching MacKencey, while two more stood across from each other. One was gesturing, using what looked like some form of sign language; the other held Mac's helmet at arm's length, slowly looking it over.

The helmet's neck band was torn and hanging down, as if it had been crudely cut away from the armor's chest section. The beast then rolled it over to look at the top, shaking it sharply.

"*Chyort!*" Kotov shouted as MacKencey's head dropped from the open end, dangling in place from the wires of his comhood. A stream of steel darts suddenly lanced out at the creatures. He opened fire and rushed the enemy before he realized he did so.

Bauer, not knowing what was happening, ran to catch up.

Morgan had just set up her gauss rifle with several smaller boxes acting as a platform, when the firing alert came up on her display; Kotov's, and now Bauer's, icons flashed. She knelt behind her weapon and activated its stabilizers, while bringing its electro-optical targeting scopes on line. The weapon's view of the world now dominated her display; quickly she swung it onto Kotov's icon.

"Twenty power, maximum light-amp." As the scene came into view, Kotov was partially blocked by a wall, while Bauer seemed to be moving in among several bodies. Morgan had felt MacKencey die, so she didn't need any confirmation; but now at the sight of his mangled armor, she had to fight to keep her emotions down. "Your friends need you," she reminded herself. "Stay sharp."

"Get Mac," Kotov said, panting from the adrenalin rush; he leveled his weapon at the gap in the wall as he watched for other possible threats.

Bauer tried to get a handle on what just happened, as he slung his weapon and started clearing the bodies away. The bad guys were heavy, making them difficult to lift, so he just dragged them clear from MacKencey by whatever body part was handy.

"Sergeant, status," Ingram said over the comm.

"Sir, we found Mac. Negative," Kotov answered the unasked question. "We have engaged and terminated five unknowns."

"And Ma'Rou?"

"Nothing yet."

"I'll be there shortly," Ingram said.

After dragging the last one off by its arm, Bauer now saw the carnage that had been wreaked on his friend. In the back of his mind, something didn't make sense. Looking around he found his answer. "Sergei," he called out.

"*Da?*"

"These things didn't use small arms." Bauer stepped over one of the bodies to reach down to draw up its arm. Held in a death grip by its four-fingered hand was a stylized axe. The blade was broad, and narrowed down to form a buckler over the grip; opposing the blade was a long, thick spike.

The snap of a passing bullet startled the men. Nearby something fell, and fell hard.

"They're coming over the top!" Morgan yelled over the comm, as she rained down gauss darts on the enemy still out of sight atop the one-story structure to their left. Some rounds struck the glass but it must have been tempered as it dimpled but did not shatter.

Kotov back-stepped away and quickly opened up his field of fire. Standing next to MacKencey's body, Bauer retrieved his weapon.

Now at the ready, all Kotov heard were the sounds of metal smashing into armor, and the thuds of bodies. *No screams of pain, not even the yells of an infantry charge*, he thought. "But I know you can die, you *sukinsyn!*" he said, as his fear turned into the need for bloody vengeance.

As the first of them boiled over the top, Kotov opened up at full cyclic; the magnetic rails of his gauss rifle hummed with surging power as multiple darts entered and exited the tracks simultaneously at supersonic velocity.

Kotov swung the weapon using the stream of fire like the teeth of a chainsaw. The armor-piercing darts punched through the attacker's armor, and tumbled away as they tore through flesh and smashed bone. Now spinning at odd angles, many rounds emerged from one victim only to rip into another. Most of the creatures died before they reached the ground, while Bauer—firing more selectively—picked off those remaining.

An alert tone sounded in Kotov's helmet as his ammunition counter tracked rapidly down toward zero. "I'm out!" he yelled as his weapon went dry; with a practiced hand, he released the spent drum and reached for a new one.

"Acknowledged." Bauer picked up his rate of fire.

Then as if on cue, like a cresting wave, the enemy poured over the top and pressed through the gap. It was like standing in front of an oncoming truck: every fiber of your being screams for you to run, as you just stand there and yell back *NO!* Bauer concentrated on dealing with the most immediate threats, but for each one he dropped, another one pushed past and continued to press forward. Both time and distance were running out.

With his weapon pointing downward, Kotov had just slotted the ammunition drum into its top feedway when the creatures reached him. With a slap he locked the drum home, as an accompanying tone signaled that the weapon was loading. Acting on instinct, Kotov swung his weapon up as he reached for its trigger group.

Before he could fire, an armored hand reached up and grabbed hold of the barrel's frame, attempting to wrench it free. Kotov grunted as the sudden jerk caused burning pains across his shoulders and chest.

"Sergei?" Bauer called, as he stole a quick glance; Kotov was being overrun. Bauer turned and fired; both darts hit home, dropping the attacker. As he swung back, the first blow struck him in the abdomen, somehow managing to punch deep through his body armor. In that instance, the ancient part of Bauer's brain kicked in, shifting reality into slow motion as survival hormones surged through him.

He wanted—he *needed*—to react, but couldn't. He heard the medium gauss rifle buzzing off in the distance, as darts poured out of the weapon so quickly the individual sounds blended together. He then knew the truth of his situation: although men fought together, they died alone.

Kotov struggled for control of his weapon as the creatures swarmed him. Screaming with the effort, he forced the weapon's muzzle down toward the ground; the impacting darts threw out a wave of splinters, causing several of the creatures to jump away. Pivoting, he brought the weapon up, still firing. At point-blank range, the force of impact shattered the darts into blazing bits of glowing metal as they danced over the creature's armor.

"Bauer, fall back!" Kotov shouted.

No response.

"Bauer!" As he looked to his right, a new red death marker appeared among a group of creatures. "*Chyort!*" he yelled as he brought his weapon around hard and cut them down.

Something smashed into his helmet, making the left side of his face go numb. Turning in the direction of the blow, he hosed down the creatures rushing him. The demons danced as they were torn apart by his murderous fire.

"Now..." he started to say to his fallen comrade, as something hit him hard in the lower back. It burned like a red-hot piece of metal. It was like someone had thrown a switch; his legs would not bear him and he fell over, dragged down by the weight of his weapon.

He lost contact with himself as shock set in. Beyond his rapidly fading world, he faintly heard his suit's Pacscomp. He could not understand what it was saying—then its neutral voice boomed directly into his mind.

"Your situation is critical; Engaging Combat," the automatic system psicommed.

Kotov reared up, pulling in a deep lungful of air as cardiac stimulates and synthetic hormones ignited the cells throughout his body; his mind cleared and his vision sharpened to a high contrast. He tried to get up, but could only manage to bring himself up on his elbows. He looked back over his shoulder; the enemy soldier stood there, one hand still holding whatever it used to kill him. The creature put one foot on Kotov's back, driving him down; with a yank, it pulled the weapon free. It stood there, hefting in both hands what appeared to be a larger version of the hand axe; the six-inch spiked end wet with blood.

"Not like this!" Kotov cursed. "Suit-mode—"

Morgan continued to pick off targets as Kotov fell out of view behind the wall, leaving only his superimposed icon; Ingram now came into view as he approached Kotov's position.

"Morgan, what's...?" Ingram said as there was a brief warning flash around Kotov's icon. The explosion was fierce. Its pressure wave wrenched bone and metal and glass alike into lethal fragments that flew out to find other victims. Face down against the container, Morgan felt the shockwave passing through the tower, followed by the boom. She opened her eyes; her scopes showed that where two of her friends had recently stood there lay only carnage.

In the foreground, Ingram stood up; Morgan shifted her weapon to cover him. "Sir, are you all right?"

"I'm in one piece. Are there any more of them?" he asked.

Morgan panned across the scene. "Sir, nothing's moving over there. In fact, I'm not even getting their death markers," she said, wondering why she felt nothing at the words.

"Kotov command-detonated his grenades. That would have fried what was left of their comm-gear," he said. "I'm falling back to your position."

"Acknowledged." Morgan zoomed out the scopes to take in a larger area.

Ingram bounced along at a fast jog some five meters from the edge of the drop off. As he passed a cluster of containers something ran out.

"Sir!" Morgan yelled as she zoomed in; several of those things—axes held high—were heading for him. There was no time for an aimed shot. As her targeting reticle's pip crossed the attacker, Morgan fired. In an explosion of armor, the first one went down; she shifted to the next and fired. Her rounds slammed into the creature but off center. It kept moving, one arm smoking but not out of action.

Ingram turned and opened up as the last two closed to within just a few meters of him; one ran right behind the other. He caught the closest one in a hailstorm of gauss fire, but the other used the body as a shield to gain that last meter. The thing came in low and drove its shoulder up and into Ingram's gut like a linebacker, forcing him back, off balance, half-carrying him toward the edge.

Morgan hesitated as the two forms collided, but it was obvious what the thing intended—*Shoot!* someone screamed. Her index and middle finger depressed the weapon's electronic trigger; with a crack, the dart cut through the air, leaving a distorted wake behind it.

It struck; the thing toppled forward still holding Ingram. Both went over the edge, disappearing into the black.

The targeting reticle still hovering over the spot. Morgan stared in disbelief as her emotions threatened to overwhelm her.

Then the lights came on overhead.

Automatically, the Pacscomp disengaged her light-amp and switched to day-view. The brilliantly lit world around her was at once familiar, but yet somehow beyond her ability to imagine.

The sun was barely up when Greg pulled in to the shopping center that housed Between Books. At this hour the place was care-worn and deserted, but later he would be lucky to grab time for a breath, let alone a pipe. He glanced toward the store; Laura waited for him beneath the overhang. They had some inventory to take care of before things got busy. With a sigh, he slipped out of the car. On his way across the parking lot he placed the stem of his pipe between his lips and lit up, watching the black cherry-scented smoke swirl in contrast against the fog. He only had time for a couple of puffs before putting it out again, but it was enough.

"Hey." A sleepy-eyed Laura nodded vaguely in his direction as he came up.

"Morning," Greg said, moving past her to unlock the door and flick on the lights. "Thanks for coming in early." He left her up front as he hurried in to disable the alarm. As he was moving down the aisle, his foot came down on something hard. It nearly sent him to the floor, but he caught himself on the counter.

"Ah, crap!" Greg limped toward the keypad, getting there in time to punch in his code just before the alarm sounded.

"You okay?"

"Yeah...yeah, I'm fine." He made his way back to where he'd stumbled and bent down to find a mangled Hellion figurine beside an ADF Special Forces action figure.

"What the hell?" His tongue ran along the back of his bottom lip as he considered them. "Hey, Laura," he called out. "Last night, did you see anyone fooling around over here?"

She peeked her head around the bookshelf and her eyebrow quirked as she spied him still crouched on the floor. "No, why?"

"Someone's been into the action figures." He straightened up, holding the Alliance Archives action figure. "They're to Mike's new role-playing game. We'd better keep an eye out for shoplifters. In the meantime, put this one and the others in the locked case." He handed her the Ingram character and tossed the mangled Hellion into the trash can before heading to the back and the new stock waiting to be shelved.

It moved at a slow pace down the valley that ran between the cliff-like structures making up this place; the top of its head rode past some twenty meters below the edge of the drop-off she felt each of its steps as a dull thump beneath her.

Confusion and a growing feeling of helplessness replaced her grief. Frustration at her inability to help her friends screamed through her. "Well, Stonebridge, what sage advice do you have for me now?" she said to the ghost of her past, her only solid memory outside of the squad. Again, memory failed her.

She felt the vibration of several thumps as something landed at her back. Her heart felt like it would blow out of her chest; she knew there was no room to fight, let alone a place to hide. She spun, reaching for her sidearm.

With the weapon halfway out of its holster, she stopped. Standing there without his helmet was Ma'Rou; his left eye wept and part of his ear was torn; blood caked the side of his furry face and ran down his shoulder armor.

Morgan pressed her sidearm back into the holster. She dropped to her knees and reached out for the Parr. Ma'Rou limped to Morgan, who gently picked him up into her arms.

"Suit-mode, external." She activated the suit's exterior speakers. "You look like shit," she said in a laughing tone; tears welled up in her eyes. "Can you travel?"

Without his Pacscomp, Ma'Rou was reduced to what the Parr called the "monkey nods." As he signaled yes, Morgan gently lifted him up toward her shoulder, where he worked his way back onto her pack.

She stood up carefully and retrieved her gauss rifle, which she then slung across her chest. Turning, she looked in the direction the giant—for lack of a better term—had gone. A city-sized field of colorful containers, punctuated by a multitude of bizarre objects stretched before her.

She had to rescue Ingram. "You set?" She heard two taps on the back of her helmet; with that she started the climb down.

Every war produces its fair share of wounded, both mental and physical. They are the inevitable byproduct of the battlefield. Some wounds heal quickly and completely. Others take longer, if they ever heal at all, leaving the bearer broken in some way. The lengths a society goes to attempting to make them whole again speaks volumes about the character of the culture that put them in harm's way.

Greg Schauer

BROTHERS

Danielle Ackley-McPhail

T̲HEY TOLD ME THE DOG'S NAME, BUT DON'T BOTHER TO ASK WHAT IT IS. I IGNORED them. I'm good at that; retreating deep into the core of my thoughts where they cannot touch me. Where I cannot hear such things as names. You see, they taught me well in Basic. Names mean something. Names make things personal. Personal is important.

I've had enough of names. Life's easier when nothing matters. I turn it off, the way I've been trained. With nothing left to fight, or fight for, I retreat to my fallback position. I fill my world with the faceless, the nameless. I can ignore what doesn't matter. I tell myself that's everything.

Buried deep in my heart, a still, small voice calls me a liar.

Me. I tell it to shut the fuck up.

The soldier sat in the center of the room, back straight, flat eyes staring off into the middle distance, arms folded carefully in his lap so that no portion of his body touched the frame of the power-chair any more than necessary. Other than the occasional tic across the blade of his cheek and breath so shallow it barely expanded his chest, the man did not move. Just outside of kicking range lay a golden retriever, body position projecting non-aggression as its eyes remained locked on the soldier's face. Mirroring the man, the dog scarcely moved, but for anxious little twitches of its brow. Occasionally, a faint whine escaped to jar the silence.

It was impossible to tell which one of them it came from.

Two men stood just outside the hospital room, watching its occupants through an observation monitor mounted beside the door. One wore captain's bars on the collar of his lab coat; the other had an eagle tacked to his chest.

"Permission to speak freely, sir?" the doctor asked.

The colonel's brow flattened in a foreboding manner, but he nodded.

"Are you certain about this, sir?"

His superior's forehead dipped lower into an actual frown as he turned sharp eyes on the doctor. "Captain?"

"I'm sorry, sir, but that man hardly seems a viable candidate for a service dog. Sure, he needs one, but I see no sign he has any interest in improving his standard of living. Hell, to be frank, sir, I don't see he cares much about living at all. He won't even sign the release for the basic prosthetic enhancements that would get him out of that chair, let alone the advanced limb regeneration you brought me on for." The doctor braced himself and pushed on despite the colonel's darkening expression. "There's not one damn thing I can do for him without his cooperation. When I think of how many soldiers are still waiting to rebuild their lives...men and women who are desperate for a chance like this..." His voice trailed off and only by extreme effort did he keep from gulping back his unspoken words.

The colonel pivoted and stepped into his personal space. "And if that was you in that chair? Would you want us to give up on you because your head wasn't in the right place?"

Shame drained the doctor's cheeks of color. His back straightened and he gave a sharp shake of his head.

"We don't give up on our own, Captain. Is that understood? In my infantry days, we shouldered our brother's burden when he struggled to press forward. This is no different. There are two heroes in that room and neither one of them deserves to fall through the cracks because someone else didn't have the patience to give them time to sort themselves out."

"But he won't even acknowledge the dog!" the doctor's frustration overcame his sense of military protocol. "We're wasting everyone's time—sir..."

"If we give up, we've already failed."

In the distance, the sound of mortar rounds and soldiers screaming grows louder. Gunfire shreds the air. My arms jerk, struggling to raise an absent rifle and return fire. What's left of my legs burn with the need to run. Toward the fighting? Away? Who can say...? Neither one is possible. My jaw clenches tight enough I swear I feel the teeth shift in their sockets as my head falls back. The memories of combat claw their way along every nerve until my body shakes with equal violence. If my chest held any breath, it would have machine-gunned out in sobs. Good thing the flashbacks leave me breathless.

A familiar ripple runs up the edge of my jaw, jarring me out of the nightmare. I lay there, stunned, as a gentle, but urgent *woof* whispers across my bonejack, the subvocal communications device the military had embedded in my jaw. I didn't realize the dog and I had anything in common, let alone military-issue hardware. I'm so stunned that I scarcely realize I've sat up. The first I've done so on my own since being dragged in pieces off the front line.

My gaze scans the semi-dark of the room and I scowl as I realize I can't locate the dog. And then I hear it. A low thud rises repeatedly from the floor beside my bed. I drop down to the pillow with a snarl and turn my back to the sound. I tell myself a tail wag in the dark is nothing and bend my will to pushing the memory of the dog's face from my thoughts even as the thudding lulls me to sleep.

The doctor gritted his teeth in frustration as he came onto shift. He had put years into perfecting his skills and each day of this assignment only drove home how those skills were being wasted. He hid his resentment behind a professional expression and approached the nurses' station.

"Good morning, doctor," the day nurse greeted him as she handed him a digital tablet already displaying data from the night before. "We've had some progress. Biometrics indicates a more restful night. Only one nightmare and a couple of minor episodes. The lieutenant even sat up briefly around 2am...unassisted."

The doctor *humphed* beneath his breath. Progress, or anomaly? He stepped to the monitor outside the lieutenant's door. Skepticism twisted his lips as he stared at the familiar tableau of soldier and dog, nearly indistinguishable from each day before, but for a rhythmic twitch of the man's right hand. It appeared as if he fought a subconscious impulse to reach for a sidearm.

The remote biometric scanners embedded beneath the soldier's skin fed a steady stream of data to the monitor. Based on the elevated adrenaline and cortisol levels, paired with increased activity recorded in the amygdala and hypothalamus, a flashback gripped the patient, the twitch the only outward sign. A faint frown bowed the doctor's lips. He reached for the monitor controls, ready to administer a fast-acting sedative via the subdermal implants should the lieutenant exhibit violent behavior.

As the doctor's finger hovered over the hotkey, he spied movement on the monitor. Instinct shouted at him to jab the control releasing the sedative, until it registered that the movement came from the dog. Slowly it rose until it sat back on its haunches, eyes still locked on the soldier's face. The dog barked sharply, abrupt, jarring in the silence of the room, even through the speakers. It was a no-nonsense bark, not aggressive, not playful. Stern, the doctor would have to say, if anyone asked, like a good squad leader bringing a soldier in line. The lieutenant jerked and briefly seemed to focus, his eyes tracking with precision on the dog. They stared one another down for several long moments until the soldier scowled. The dog merely stared calmly back, slowly swishing its tail against the tile floor. Then the moment ended. The dog lay down and the soldier went back to staring off into space, his hand no longer twitching toward a holster that wasn't there.

The doctor stepped away, feeling something akin to embarrassment, as if he'd spied on something private. Pensive, he went about his rounds, his inner cynic refusing to put much store in the incident while his inner optimist cheered.

I wake up to the stench of blood, cordite, and piss and I'm damned if I can tell if the smells are real. All I can be certain of is the silky head wedging itself beneath my shaking hand. I yank my fingers into a fist, pulling away, only to have a moist tongue swipe lightly across my knuckles. Jerking myself upright to get further away, I glare into the gloom, my eyes slowly adjusting to the low light of the one remaining monitor as my chest continues to heave in the aftermath of night terrors.

A subtle shift in the texture of the darkness to my nine shows me the dog's position. The edge of the bed completely obscures its body, all except for the head. I can just see the outline of its muzzle resting on the mattress. I growl, primal and deep from my belly, warning it away from my territory. An all-too-human sigh answers my aggression, followed by a soft thud, as the dog lays back down on the floor, nails gently scraping against the tiles as it curls up to sleep.

Something that might be guilt twists in my gut. I shut it off, crushing the blankets in my fist as I hump my ass forward until I drop flat to my back. Pain sends sparks across my vision as rough, institutional-grade cotton strafes across what's left of my legs. I'm glad of it. The pain feeds the anger, killing any other emotion that dares raise its head. Just as well.

I refuse to feel grateful to a fucking dog.

That's what I tell myself as I pursue sleep with the same grim determination with which I used to approach an enemy line.

"Do you see that?" the colonel greeted him as he came out of his patient's room. The doctor pivoted, expecting to see some monumental change, some sudden breakthrough between the time he turned to leave and when he walked through the door. His eyes, doubly trained for observation, spied nothing.

"What, sir?"

The colonel's head slowly nodded with satisfaction. "The dog...he's lying closer."

Dumbfounded, the doctor watched his superior stroll away.

I wake in the night to the sound of whimpers and for a humiliating moment I think they are coming from me. Shame sends the bitter taste of bile surging to my throat. Then I hear a sudden thrashing from beside the bed and I know for once the weakness is not mine.

Not for the first time, I curse that I am no longer equipped to kick. Nearly as frustrating is the realization that there is nothing within reach I'm willing to throw, given the impossibility of independent retrieval. I lie there glaring at where I know the ceiling to be. I won't allow myself to feel enough to be angry or annoyed; but, as whines begin to join the thrashing, I carefully rotate onto my belly toward the edge of the bed and smack at the pain-in-the-ass dog. My hand comes down on its flank, tangling in long, sweaty strands of hair.

How the hell does a dog manage to feel clammy?

My instinct is to yank, but what I feel beneath that coat startles me. By touch I identify a familiar texture, knots and ropes of intruding scars where smooth muscle should be. The flesh beneath my fingers shudders, involuntary movements that I myself suffer. The dog's jaw snaps at the air, but nowhere near my hand. As he continues to cry, I realize the sounds are again subvocal, transmitting across my bonejack.

I don't want to feel kinship. I don't want to feel a thing. And yet my hand, of its own accord, strokes the damn dog and that fucking voice deep inside of me hums with satisfaction as the thrashing slows, then stops, and no more sounds ripple along my jaw to echo deep in my ear.

For a moment in the dark, I leave my hand resting on the dog's flank to feel the returning warmth, finding peace in fighting off nightmares, even if they aren't my own. Then I flinch as I realize what I'm doing. I shove away from the connection and roll over onto my back. I commence glaring up at the ceiling as I tell myself I am not listening for the sounds of returning nightmares the way I'd been trained to listen for covert activity on patrol.

I have my own demons to battle. The dog is on its own.

An orderly with corporal markings on his collar grabbed the next chart in his assignment slot. He sighed as he saw the patient. Not that it surprised him. New to this posting, he drew the shit assignments and this was the worst one. Time to take the lieutenant to his therapy session.

Man, this one is screwed up, the orderly thought. He had to wonder why they didn't house him in the psych wing to begin with. The routine was already too familiar: wrestle him into the chair and escort him down the hall, leave him for an hour in the head shrinker's office, then back again. And never once did the guy even blink, let alone spill his guts.

It was like that sometimes. The bodies came home, but the spirits remained trapped on the battlefield.

"Time to go for a ride." He started to manhandle the patient into his chair. It was no easy task. Even with bits of him missing, the guy was dense, heavy with muscle not yet gone soft. On top of that, the orderly suspected he purposely went dead weight, making the task harder than it needed to be. The soldier hissed as his left stump smacked into the lowered bed rail, but made no effort to cooperate, his gaze still fixed on nothing, though his facial muscles tensed and a faint hint of satisfaction seemed to gleam deep in his eyes.

The orderly cursed and struggled to pull the soldier closer to the chair. "Come on, man, cut it out and help me here..."

Again—completely unintentional—flesh met metal.

Suddenly, the orderly froze as he felt pointed teeth pierce his scrubs, though not his flesh. He looked down to find the dog's jaws gripping his ankle. A rumbling growl slowly filled the room. Before he could react, the door opened and the doctor hurried in, a second orderly behind him.

"Sergeant, stand down," the doctor ordered. The first orderly looked up, confused, until the jaws gripping his ankle released. The dog sat back at attention with a slight snarl curling his muzzle, but made no further sound.

The doctor shifted his gaze toward the bed and continued, this time more sternly. "Lieutenant, get in the chair." As he spoke, the second orderly came around the side of the bed to assist. He wasn't needed.

The soldier set his jaw and jerked away from the orderly's grip. He pivoted on the edge of the bed and yanked the wheelchair so he could slide over the back into place. His arms went taut with the effort and his movements were the slightest bit awkward, but capable.

Moments later, they were back on schedule and ready to deploy.

They want me to talk. I want them to leave me the fuck alone. What right do they have to know the hell I've been through? A soldier doesn't show weakness. A soldier doesn't hand the enemy a weapon to use against him. I have learned to treat everyone as an enemy. That way it's safer if I'm wrong.

Enemy... Friend... Either way, I won't share my demons with them.

They wheel me away from my cell, down long, featureless beige hallways, and into a butter-yellow room I suspect is meant to lull me. Fat chance. I retreat within myself once more as the psych doc starts his usual chatter. Only distantly do I hear the words he says. Again talking of focal points and mantras, then extolling the virtue of meditation. And finally, the need to purge the darkness...to expose my memories, even if only to myself.... Each time, I stare a hole into his forehead until he gives up. He speaks, as he has before, of the benefits of reconstructive surgery and physical therapy. I briefly surface from the depths to slam him with a glare.

The bastard doesn't even seem to notice. He grips my shoulder and tells me to have a good day.

The psych doc has a death wish, only I'm helpless to deliver. My jaw grinds at the private admission. The orderly is wheeling me out of the door before I can peel back the layers of cold indifference enough to respond.

A faint ticking sounds behind me. It takes me a moment to recognize the dog's nails tapping an irregular rhythm on the floor as he shadows us. If I cared more, I'd order them to take the mutt away. I tell myself it's not important.

That fucking voice calls me a liar.

On third shift, sudden darkness engulfed the hospital wing housing long-term care. For a split second, total silence reigned as the usual symphony of monitors and machines and quietly bustling personnel abruptly halted. The briefest instance of chaos gave way to well-trained responses as the staff secured the floor and checked on each patient.

At the nurses' station, the charge nurse answered the emergency comm as security called in for a sit-rep. "Total loss of power," she reported. "Emergency generators are non-responsive. The wing has been secured."

"Acknowledged. Engineering is already aware of the malfunction. They are working to restore main power and repair the defective unit. Are any of your patients at risk?"

Sudden screams from one of the rooms interrupted the charge nurse before she could respond.

I watch them die tonight. Everyone. The ones I rescued. The ones I couldn't get to in time. Soldiers I haven't seen since my first tour of duty. Everyone I know. Even the fucking dog. I'm left alone in total darkness. My mind screams at me this is wrong but it's overwhelmed by the sounds of the dying. The cries go on forever and my nose shuts down in defense against the sweet, acrid stench of blood and death and spent ordnance.

There is a sound to my three o'clock; a faint click, followed by the careful steps of soft-shod feet making an effort not to be heard. My combat instincts go on alert, muscles tense and my breathing drops into a steady, ready rhythm. I curse the dark, even as my hindbrain tries to tell me there should be light. A faint glow instead of unending black. More noises come across the intervening distance distracting me from what should and should not be. Without thought, I slowly edge myself up, bracing for attack. The sounds of the line gradually filter through the background. A growl rumbles across my 'jack. I run the blade of my hand over the ground looking for my rifle, a grenade, hell, even a pistol, but I'm left with only my hands. I move to crouch, ready to launch myself at the enemy creeping up.

Something doesn't feel right. My balance is off. I try to compensate, only to fall backward, my head thudding against something hard and metallic. I catch myself before I land on my back again. There is a gasp in the darkness as I shake my head to clear the fog. The intruder hurries forward, no longer making an effort to be silent. My jaw clamps down and my fingers curl into powerful claws. I feel capable of tearing muscle from bone. As the darker patch of shadow moves closer there is a faint glimmer. Low, like the moon's reflection. Or a shielded light.

I bunch my muscles to launch myself at the target. My lips twist in a silent snarl as a battle cry builds in my chest ready to be unleashed. I don't forget that everyone's dead. That I'm alone to face this unknown enemy. One of how many? As I push off I let loose a roar.

Even as a piercing, feminine shriek rises from mere feet away, something comes at me from the opposite side. I fail to counteract the assault as my attacker slams across my chest from low and to my left. I'm thrown back, a heavy weight pinning me to ground much softer than it should be.

First comes a sharp, commanding bark, then warning growls rumble beside my right ear. What seems like a supernova explodes the darkness as a distant *thunk* and *whir* penetrate my haze. The monitor beside what I now realize is my bed flares to life revealing one of the nurses, pale and trembling in the sudden glow. Behind her, several orderlies hurry through the door.

I barely notice as I my eyes lock on the damned dog weighing down my chest.

Slowly, the dog angles its head until its eyes lock with mine. If I look past the fur, it's like looking into the mirror. The ghosts of familiar horrors drift behind its gaze. *His* gaze... He doesn't make another sound. He doesn't have to. My heart stutters as I realize what I've almost done. My hands come up reflexively to wrap around the dog, clutching him to my chest as I accept the truth.

He saved her.

He saved *me*.

I recognize the power of names even as my heart calls him Brother.

My head drops back on the flattened pillow and I struggle to breathe as the woman scrambles from the room, completely forgetting whatever brought her into the devil's den to begin with. I wait for the sound of the orderlies filing out behind her. I wait for what I know I must do, though my instincts scream *No!*

They want me to talk? So I will talk, but not to them. I lay there in the darkness with a warm mound now stretched out beside me. Absently, I stroke the dog's gnarled flank and his tail gently thumps the bed. I don't make a sound anyone but the dog can hear. Instead, over the bonejack I whisper the horrors I have seen. Done. Been unable to prevent. I admit my sense of helplessness. My feelings of failure. The pillow is drenched with tears beneath my head as I battle for my life. Pain pours from my heart like blood from a wound. Cleansing. Healing. Purging.

By the time dawn tints the sky I have survived the first engagement of my on-going war.

ABOUT THE AUTHORS

Award-winning author and editor Danielle Ackley-McPhail has worked both sides of the publishing industry for longer than she cares to admit. In 2014 she joined forces with husband Mike McPhail and friend Greg Schauer to form her own publishing house, eSpec Books. Her published works include six novels, Yesterday's Dreams, Tomorrow's Memories, Today's Promise, The Halfling's Court, The Redcaps' Queen, and Baba Ali and the Clockwork Djinn, written with Day Al-Mohamed. She is also the author of the solo collections A Legacy of Stars, Consigned to the Sea, Flash in the Can, and Transcendence, the non-fiction writers' guide, The Literary Handyman, and is the senior editor of the Bad-Ass Faeries anthology series, Gaslight & Grimm, Dragon's Lure, and In an Iron Cage. Her short stories are included in numerous other anthologies and collections.

Author and graphic artist Mike McPhail is member of the Military Writers Society of America; he is dedicated to helping his fellow service members (and those deserving civilians) in their efforts to become authors/editors/ artist, as well as supporting related organization in their efforts to help those "who have given their all for us."
www.milscifi.com

His love of science, technology, and developing an understanding of the human condition play an important role in his writing, art, and game design, all of which are built upon his training as an aeronautical engineer and dreams of becoming a NASA mission specialist, balanced by his enlistment in the service.

www.mikemcphail.com

In the late 80s he was involved in game design, namely the Martial Role-Playing Game (All'Arc MRPG), a manual-based, hardcore military science fiction adventure, set in his Alliance Archives universe; sections of which are being reissued under the title of From The Archives (FT'Arc) by AGM Publications, a division of eSpec Books, LLC.

He is best known as the editor and illustrator of the award-winning Defending The Future series of military science fiction anthologies, which just celebrated its tenth anniversary with its Best Of... collection, and the continuation of the series.

www.defendingthefuture.com

In 2014 he added the title of publisher, as the co-founder of eSpec Books LLC, Electronic Speculative Fiction Publishing.

www.especbooks.com

ABOUT THE EDITOR

Greg Schauer has been a bookseller for over 33 years as the owner of Between Books in Claymont Delaware. He has also helped produce concerts by local and national bands at the Arden Gild Hall in Arden Delaware, one of the country's oldest continuously run secular utopian art colonies, for the past 10 years. He has previously worked on Stories in Between: the Between Books 30th anniversary anthology with W.H. Horner and Jeanne Benzel, Steam-powered Tales of Awesomeness Vol 1 by Brian Thomas and Ray Witte, With Great Power with John L. French, and The Society for the Preservation of CJ Henderson with Danielle Ackley-McPhail. He can be contacted at gschauer@betweenbooks.com.

Kickstarter Troops

Adam Selby-Martin
Alain Fournier
Alan Danziger
Anders M. Ytterdahl
Andreas Gustafsson
Andrew Hatchell
Andrew J Clark IV
Angela Carlson
Ann Stolinsky
Anonymous
Anonymous Reader
Anton Kukal
Aramanth Dawe
Arthur W. Lobdell
Ashley Knight
Ayelet Benson
Barbara and Carl Kesner
Brenda Cooper
Brendan Lonehawk
Brent Millis
Brian Bishop
Brian 'Commodore Stargazer' Whitcraft
Bryan Geddes
Candace R. Benefiel
Carol Ann Kukal
Cathy Franchett
Chad Bowden
Chand Svare Ghei chasvag.com
Charles Anchors
Cheri Kannarr
Chris Volcheck
Colin Lloyd
Curtis & Maryrita Steinhour

Dave Hermann
Dave Lewis
David McDermott
David Mortman
Dorothy O'Hare
D-Rock
edward zagadinow
eerian sadow
Erin Penn
Evaristo Ramos, Jr.
Fan of Words
Fran Stewart
Gareth Pendleton
Gavran
Glenn Goldman
GMark Cole
Greg Resnik
Guy McLimore
Hamel Moric
Hiram G Wells
Holly Hunt
Ian Harvey
Isaac 'Will It Work' Dansicker
Ivan Donati
J.R. Murdock
Jakub Narebski
James Chambers
James Rowland
James W. Armstrong-Wood
Janine K. Spendlove
Janito Vaqueiro Ferreira Filho
Jason F. Broadley
Jason Genser
Jason Russell

Jay Zastrow
Jessica Enfante
Jessica Reid
Jiri "Picky" Cerny
John "Shadowcat" Ickes
John G. Hartness
John Green
John Idlor
John L. French
Joyce Ann Garcia from McAllen Texas
Judy Waidlich
JW
Karen and James Henson
Karl Gallagher
Keith Hall
Keith Tracton
Keith West, Future Potentate of the Solar System
Kelly Farmer
Ken Mencher
Kerry aka Trouble
Lady Ozma
Lark Cunningham
Lauren Hoffman
Laurie Gailunas
Laurie Hicks
Lennhoff Family
Lisa Kruse
Louise Lowenspets
Louise McCulloch
M A Pugliese
M. L. Falkenstein
M. Menzies
Marc "mad" Winkelmann
Margaret St. John
Mark Knapp Jr
Mark Lukens

Martin Bernstein
Mary Spila
Mat Masding-Grouse
Matt P
Matthew Hieb
Max Kaehn
mdtommyd
Michael Carson
Michael D Blanchard
Michael Fedrowitz
Michael Skolnik
Mike Maurer
Nathan Duby
Nathan Turner
Neil A Ottenstein
Nellie B.
Nicole McPherson
Niki Coppola
Pat Hayes
Patrick Thomas
Paul Ryan
Paul van Oven
Pepita Hogg-Sonnenberg
Peter Thew
Peter Young
R.T. Bryson
Ralph M. Seibel
Raymond Finch
Revek
RK Bookman
Rob Karp
Robby Thrasher
Robert E Waters
Roisin mcCormac
Ross Hathaway
Roy Romasanta
S Ruskin
sam murphy

Samuel Lubell
Scott A Johnson
Scott Elson
Scott Mayanrd
Scott Schaper
Sean McGarry
Sebastian H.
ShadowCub
Shervyn
Sheryl R. Hayes
Silence in the Library Publishing
Simo Muinonen
Simon Clark
Soldier Systems Daily
Stephanie Lucas
Stephen A, Fender
Stephen Ballentine
Stephen Cheng
Suragai
Susan Carlson
Susan R Grossman

Svend Andersen
SwordFire
Tamara Michelle Slaten
thatraja
The loyal minion, Linda
Thomas M. Karwacki Jr.
Thomas Werner
Tina England
Tina Noe Good
Tom Berrisford
Tomas Burgos-Caez
Tony Finan
Tory Shade
Towelman
V. Hartman DiSanto
Vickie B
Wallace MacBix
Wes Rist
William Hughes
William Wiebking